SWEET DECEMBER

A Silver Fox Resort Novel

LYZ KELLEY

Belvitri LLC

About Sweet December

A thirty-year pact is about to expire, and it's time to pay up.

Melissa Davenport achieved her dream of becoming the first female US fighter pilot by putting romance on hold. But when Brian Newburg, her smart, sexy engineering study-buddy, asks what she's doing for her fiftieth birthday, she remembers their college pact.

If neither is married by their fiftieth birthdays, they will get married.

After a fulfilling stint at NASA, Brian now works as an aerodynamic engineer. His career path is about to change though, and he wants hard-as-nails General Davenport to join him on a new adventure.

Melissa isn't eager to leave a career she sacrificed all for behind, but Brian still makes her heart pound.

Join Melissa and Brian as they discover the magical powers of the Silver Fox Resort in this second chance romance.

Chapter 1

A light tap on the frame of her open office door pulled Melissa Davenport out of her brainstorming notes for how to impress the brass at the next joint meeting. She looked at the list of three items, sighed, and massaged her fingers over the back of her neck.

Her current assignment wasn't bad. In fact, being the commander of the Air Force Recruiting Service Center was pretty darn good. The problem? She was bored. Flying jets was a whole lot more fun than pushing papers.

"Hey, Boss." Tammy Parker, one of the handful of senior female officers at the Joint Base in San Antonio, paused, frowning. "You look distracted. Am I interrupting?"

Melissa attempted a casual laugh. "I was just admiring the view and thinking it'd be a great day for a run."

The sky was a cloudless, crisp blue for November. The winds were calm, and the flying conditions perfect, which added even more fuel to her melancholy. She wanted to fly, not spend her days grounded in buildings constructed for function, not aesthetics.

Tammy's eyes flicked to the base view outside Melissa's

large office window. "Agreed. Any day that isn't hotter than a hundred and twenty is good. I take it you missed your run this morning."

"Meetings," was all she needed to say. A bubble of laughter eased the tension in Melissa's neck and shoulders.

Like her, Tammy had served multiple tours in Afghanistan and Iraq. Of all the conditions that made deployment duty almost unbearable, the scorching heat was the worst, especially when decked out in full kit. Sand was next in line. It found its way into everything from her bed, to her equipment, to her boots. Nothing escaped.

But here, completing her daily five-mile run in the mild, seventy-degree weather, on a smooth running trail, with clean running shoes, was—literally—a breeze. August, when summer heat and humidity peaked, wasn't quite as pleasant, but most days, being stationed at JBSA was better than The Sandbox.

"By the way," Tammy leaned a forearm against the doorjamb, "the General is asking for last month's recruiting numbers. They're not due until next week, but she's meeting with the funding committee tomorrow and thinks an updated report would be helpful."

Melissa swallowed a weary sigh. Since accepting this so-called promotion, her career had shifted from flying for the 4th Fighter Wing to navigating the complex world of military politics. Her days were filled with endless meetings, reams of paper, and projects that moved at a snail's pace—if at all. And government cuts were the bane of her existence these days.

"You miss it, don't you?" Tammy's question was soft, almost hesitant. Walking the line between friendship and professional distance wasn't easy.

"Flying? Being out on the front lines? Never knowing what the next mission will be?" Her attention slid back to the window and the endless blue expanse beyond. "Every single day." She shook off pent-up frustrations and squared her shoulders. "Tell the General she'll have her report by EOD."

"Will do." Tammy hesitated. "Some of us are meeting for happy hour tacos and margaritas at Juan's Cantina. Want me to save you a seat?"

Melissa cringed at the thought of shoulder-to-shoulder bodies packed in a bar with the sugary-sweet smell of lime, triple sec, and tequila swamping everything. "Not this time, I'm afraid."

Unfortunately, she didn't know what she *was* in the mood for. Lately her restlessness nagged at her like a half-forgotten dream, and the disquiet kept her on edge. Over the years, she'd learned to trust her instincts. This time, though, she didn't understand what that nagging feeling was trying to tell her.

"Thanks for the invite, but I have a last-minute date with a spreadsheet."

She appreciated her staff. She had a fulfilling career, good —if distant—friends, and, thanks to the phone call from her doctor three days ago, a clean bill of health. The big C wasn't going to kick her ass.

Not this time, anyway.

"If you finish up before o-dark-thirty, join us. We're celebrating Shelly's divorce." Tammy winked. "First round's on Shelly."

"Don't wait for me." Sometimes playing the boss card provided a convenient, unarguable excuse. "If I don't see you before you leave, pass along my congrats or condolences to Shelly—whichever is appropriate."

"Sure thing." Tammy got the message. "Do you want your door open or closed?"

"Closed, please. Otherwise, I'll still be grappling with this spreadsheet come Monday morning."

Like any military installation, the Air Force Recruiting

Service Center was big on protocol, rules, and regulations. The department was quiet, aside from the distant ring of phones, muted conversations, and hard-heeled dress shoes on the tiled floor. There was none of the nine-to-five drama portrayed on TV sitcoms about civilian workplaces. Even so, Melissa was grateful she could closet herself in her office... the paperwork, not so much.

She tucked the niggling sense of dissatisfaction into a mental file drawer and shoved it shut, and for the rest of the afternoon she reviewed and signed off on reports, finished the general's report, accepted meeting invitations, dictated a list of tasks for her assistant to handle on Monday, answered emails, and dealt with the myriad duties required as commander.

By the time she shut down her computer, the sun had already set.

After walking across the now almost-empty parking lot, Melissa tossed her briefcase on the passenger seat of her silver Nissan SUV, climbed behind the wheel, loosened the top button of her starched blue uniform shirt, and headed home.

The closer she got to her single-story rental, the more that bothersome dissatisfaction banged and hollered to be released. Melissa cranked up the radio and rolled down her window. Even Eric Clapton's "Layla" wasn't enough to drown out the noise in her head.

"I should have gone to Juan's," she muttered, pulling into the middle of the two-car garage. She glanced at the stainless-steel Casio chronograph watch she'd splurged on two promotions ago. "Too late now."

Next time she'd make an effort to go, no excuses. Anything would be better than sitting home alone.

Once inside, she swapped her tidy blue uniform for comfy yoga pants and a long-sleeved shirt. She combed her fingers through her super-short hair and took a second to glance in the mirror. She was still getting used to the style and was thankful most of the bald spots had filled in. After months of chemo and radiation, she was even starting to feel sexy again.

Tomorrow, she promised herself, she would run double to make up for the five miles she had skipped today. Pounding miles in the dark didn't hold much appeal, whereas a glass of Sangiovese and leftover tzatziki, pita, and gyro with a salad on the side sounded like heaven.

While the leftover meat circled in the microwave, she savored the rich scent of garlic and oregano wafting through the kitchen and filled a goblet, lifting the shimmering ruby liquid up to the light, admiring the rich hues of the wine. She took a sip and felt the tension in her shoulders melt away.

Setting a placemat on the glass-topped living room coffee table, she directed Alexa to play some Stones, then sat and pulled her laptop onto her crossed legs.

She wondered how other single, fifty-year-old women were spending their Friday nights. Were they working on homework with their kids? Snuggling with their dog? Having dinner with a new boyfriend? Some, like Shelly, who'd always expected to grow old with her soul mate, ended up single, and then became part of the over-fifty dating scene. Hanging out in nightclubs and bars or settling for a guy who'd once been another woman's problem and was now hers didn't sound like a solid idea.

Then there were women like her. So focused on career achievements that they neglected the rest of life—marriage, children, even friendships. Good grief—she didn't even have a cat.

What is up with me lately? These introspective musings about life and the choices were out of character. For so long she'd kept her eye on the prize—a career as a fighter pilot—a dream that started as a seed the day her dad was killed in a Naval training exercise her senior year of high school. Now it was mission accomplished.

Mostly.

"Suck it up, Davenport." Melissa's voice echoed off the sparsely decorated walls. She had no patience with women who whined and moaned about their lives, including herself. "Unhappy? Do something about it."

But what?

She opened Facebook to see what her friends were up to these days. The bell icon in the corner of her screen announced 27 new posts. The message icon, a speech bubble with a line that looked like the scar on Harry Potter's forehead, caught her attention.

One new message.

She moused over the messenger icon and clicked, curious about who would contact her via Facebook.

Your profile still says you're single. Our big 5-0 is coming up soon. Do you remember our pact?

She scrolled up to the profile name at top speed, and her heart tripped for a beat, then two.

Brian Newburg. Well, well. Those fun-filled college day memories flooded back. Excitement bubbled inside her at the transformation of a boring Friday night to a trip down memory lane with her best friend.

The most recent profile picture revealed he'd finally shaved off his beard. She touched the screen when she realized his reddish-blond hair—that always looked mussed, no matter how short he cut it—had now gone a snowy white. Steady blue-gray eyes that belied his penchant for practical jokes and pranks were the same. So was his long, lean runner's build, and the freckles he hated so much, and that she'd secretly adored.

It had been eight months since their last exchange, just

long enough for him to disengage from his latest project. The workaholic rarely stopped working. She realized the sentiment was like the Bugatti driver calling the McLaren driver slow, but she at least took time for PT or a girls' night out once in a while.

She touched the image of his face, remembering how sweet and supportive he was when she told him about her cancer diagnosis. He'd been the one person she could open up to—and that same open honesty had been there since the first few weeks of college their freshman year.

Both of them were there for the other, no questions asked, and most likely always would be. They were two souls adrift in the world, and in some ways they both needed that anchor. Needed to know that someone was always there, no matter how dark life got.

She hesitated, hovering over the social media icon for a moment, debating whether to open the message.

The base had strict policies about using military computers for personal stuff. And because of OpSec, she was careful about what details she disclosed on Facebook. She wasn't big on public sharing either, even though it was part of the outreach necessary to attract new recruits. But tonight, she was too tired to worry about the minor violation. Melissa tapped to open Brian's profile page.

"Mmm." She examined his latest posts with a purr of pure appreciation. Aside from dark-rimmed glasses, appealing laugh lines at the corners of his eyes, and a faded scar in the center of his chin, he looked the same—an adorable hunk.

An electronic *ding* sounded from her computer, and Melissa realized she had another message.

Are you online? Time to chat? My cell changed. A ten-digit number followed the short text.

Her stomach did a funny flip-flop. Brian was home—alone?—on a Friday night. Just like her.

She typed back, *Give me 5.*

Setting the laptop onto the couch, she made a quick trip to the bathroom, grabbed her cell phone from her bedside table, then zipped into the kitchen to get the open bottle of wine. She topped off her glass, took a hefty swallow, then poked the correct sequence of numbers.

"Is this BestE?" a warm, familiar male voice asked before the second ring.

"Is this MechE?" A girlish giggle escaped at the exchange of college nicknames. "Did you just finish a major project? Or break up with your latest? It has to be one or the other."

"How do you know it's not both?" His husky laughter created an intimate connection that physical distance and eight months of radio silence could not diminish. Gregarious, outgoing, and inherently good-natured, Brian laughed a lot. But he reserved a special laugh for her—a low, sexy rumble that communicated equal parts irritation and affection accumulated over three decades. "You never met her, so it doesn't matter. And, for the record, she broke up with me. Not the other way around."

"How long were you dating?" Picking up the conversation with Brian, even after so many months, felt like slipping on a worn pair of blue jeans: easy, comfortable, a perfect fit.

"Six months." Disappointment tinged his response.

"What happened this time?"

Brian's love life was a fascinating case study in how to avoid commitment. He didn't have a problem getting women —he had a problem keeping them. He was successful, attractive, fun, kind, interesting, ambitious—the whole package. The problem, in Melissa's opinion, was his inability to make any woman the most important thing in his life. Work always came first.

It was a repeat of college all over again.

"Her parents live in Boston. When they made a last-minute decision to come out to San Francisco for an early Thanksgiving celebration, she wanted me to cancel a presentation I was scheduled to give at Embry-Riddle in Daytona Beach so I could meet them. When I said no, she said family should come before work, and that if I didn't change my plans, I wasn't husband material. At least she got one thing right."

Melissa chortled. "There's nothing wrong with putting your dreams first. You just need to find the right woman, someone who gets that you're working to change the world. That drive is part of you. It's the air you breathe. You can't just turn it on or off." Melissa realized she was rambling, and possibly revealing too much. "Then again, the woman is right. You aren't husband material. You're just like me."

"Career *woman*. There's nothing mannish about you."

The barely-there compliment caused something in her belly to constrict. There had been times when she and Brian flirted, but it was harmless. Two friends teasing each other. Nothing that ever crossed a line or hinted at anything other than platonic affection.

Even though she might have welcomed something more than platonic affection…

"Enough about me." There was a muffled sound of movement, as if Brian was shifting to get more comfortable. "I called to see what's new with you."

"Well, I'm trying to figure out how to get my career back on track. This cancer diagnosis landed me in DNIF status"

"What's that?"

"Duties Not to Include Flying. I forget you civvies don't know all the military jargon. Anyway, my DNIF landed me in this job, which sidelined my goal of adding a couple more stars to my shoulder boards. If I had stayed in the flying wing command position, my career path might have been a little more direct. Right now, I'm working with my sponsor to figure out how to get back on track."

The curveball life had pitched her in the form of stage two breast cancer changed a lot of things, including her single-minded focus on career. She needed to eat better, exercise more. Confronting one's mortality, especially when the birthday marking half a century of existence was just around the corner, put a different spin on life. Flying, breaking glass ceilings, paving the way for other talented young women, continually testing—and exceeding—her own capabilities, defined her values and her identity, but that wasn't a hundred percent her.

"Cancer sucks. Any news about when you might be in remission?"

"I just got the all clear this week."

"Melissa! That's great news. Why didn't you call and tell me?" For a second, Brian sounded a bit hurt that she hadn't already called him.

"Literally, I just found out three days ago. Work, you know?" She exhaled slowly so he wouldn't hear. "After so many months of living under a black cloud, it's hard to believe the sun is shining again. I want to believe the bad weather has passed, but I seem unable to put away the umbrella."

He chuckled. "You always sucked at analogies." His voice dropped, becoming almost tender. "I'm so glad to hear the cancer is behind you. You don't know how many times I've wanted to come down there and…"

And what? Melissa bit her tongue to keep from asking.

"We're turning fifty." Brian sounded like he couldn't get his head around that fact. "Fifty and never married. You know what that means."

For a second, she was transported back to graduation night. She tasted tequila instead of wine, felt a humid night breeze instead of climate-controlled air from her heating/AC unit, and was twenty-two with a wide-open future instead of forty-nine with so much of life behind her.

"You can't be serious." She swallowed a mouthful of rustic, fruity tannin flavor, waiting for Brian's answer.

"Why not? It sounded like a good idea twenty-some years ago."

"We were drunk," she reminded him.

"I'm not drunk now. I've been…I've been thinking about you. A lot. Ever since you told me about the cancer. I want to see you, Melissa." His tentative tone shifted, became firmer, more serious. "My company has an executive retreat scheduled next weekend at a beautiful place right on the California coast. The Silver Fox Resort. Have you heard of it?"

"You want me to join you at a company event?" She ignored the wave of disappointment that washed over her. He wasn't inviting her to a romantic escape but a corporate gathering.

"Let me fly you out for the weekend. Everyone is bringing their significant others, so there'll be plenty of opportunities for us to spend time together. You can meet the people I work with and learn more about what I do." He paused, as if swallowing. "We can celebrate our birthdays together, and—"

"And what?" she asked, a little breathless.

"And see if it might finally be time to get married."

Chapter 2

Monday morning, Brian sauntered into his office building, humming Guns N' Roses "Sweet Child O' Mine." Halfway through the chorus, he remembered the tune was one of Melissa's all-time favorites.

Friday night, after finally convincing her to join him at Silver Fox Resort for a long-overdue reunion, he pulled up "Mel's Playlist" on his old iPod and listened to the familiar rock songs while he logged a few miles on the treadmill before crashing in front of the TV with a ham sandwich and a beer. He fell asleep watching ESPN and woke up with a crick in his neck.

The crick was still causing him problems. "Fifty sucks," he mumbled, massaging the offending muscle spasm.

"What was that?" Marty Rosenblatt, a senior manager at the Daebak Automotive Design Company and Brian's good buddy, caught up with him at the double-door entrance to the building's spacious glass and chrome foyer.

"Same ole pains. Back, hips, knees, neck. Getting old sucks." Brian opened the door and gestured for Marty to go ahead. The two men crossed the marble-tiled lobby, heading for the bank of elevators.

"Wait until you're my age." Marty snorted. "Nothing works like it's supposed to"—he glanced down—"and I mean nothing."

Brian laughed. "You know, buddy, they do have meds for such things." He gave mental thanks to the universe that most of his muscles still worked properly.

For some reason, working equipment made him think of Melissa.

His gut tightened at the thought of holding her, touching her, caressing her in a way that went way beyond friendship, far beyond what he dreamed of in college but never had the guts to try. He didn't want to ruin the relationship he had with his best friend. Still didn't. He needed to tread lightly.

"Looking forward to the retreat?" Marty pushed a four-button code on the pad, and the polished steel doors slid together. "Theresa talked about the event all weekend. She has spa treatments booked every day, bought new workout gear for sunrise yoga on the beach, and spent five hundred dollars on a dress for the executive dinner. I'm glad Daebak is footing the bill for everything else, otherwise my bank account would be hurting."

Brian liked Theresa Rosenblatt, Marty's better half. He'd met her several times at cookouts, Super Bowl parties, and company picnics, and the woman deserved a weekend getaway for putting up with Marty's late nights and working weekends. She was a saint and an inspiration.

She and Marty had four teenagers, all of whom Theresa homeschooled. She coordinated a community garden that supplied organic produce to local food banks and was a best-selling author of children's books.

Brian tried to imagine how Melissa would fit in with Theresa and the other spouses. There was no shortage of accomplished men and women in that group, but none of them flew F-15s.

"I've heard the resort is incredible." Brian watched the numbers light up as the elevator rose. "The relaxed atmosphere will make it easier to approach the Japanese VIPs about moving me to the Austin plant. There's an opening for VP of the Global Environmental Program that would be a nice step up."

The elevator doors opened, revealing a hallway carpeted in plush maroon Saxony and lined with floor-to-ceiling glass-fronted offices. The two men turned left, continuing the conversation.

"What does Austin have that we don't?" Marty gave him a bemused look. "San Francisco is amazing. The food, the scenery, Napa Valley…need I say more?"

"The traffic, the cost of living, the earthquakes." Brian chuckled. "I love living in the Bay area, but that doesn't mean a change of scenery wouldn't do me some good." Besides, Melissa would only be a little over an hour away…that is, until her next assignment.

If he was going to act, he needed to act quickly.

"What then?" Marty's eyes narrowed as his mouth curved into a knowing smile. "It's a woman, isn't it? Oh, no. Don't tell me you're going after a woman."

"Maybe." Brian paused outside his office and patted his pal on the shoulder. "If you're nice, I'll introduce you. She's coming to the retreat."

"Man, you know you and women don't connect. You're too selfish with your time."

That's not true. Or is it?

Marty followed him instead of heading to his own office a bit farther down the hall. "You just broke up with," he snapped his fingers, trying to remember Brian's last girlfriend's name.

"Trish."

"That's right, Trish. See? You go through so many I can't keep up. You must have women on standby so when one relationship doesn't work out, the next one moves to the front of the line."

Brian's face heated. "C'mon, man. You know it's not like that."

Good thing he never told Marty about hiring a dating manager who arranged once-a-week coffee dates that ended when he met Trish. He thought the real estate broker and he might work out…until he wouldn't cancel his work plans.

He wanted to get married, settle down, have someone to go home to at the end of the day. He'd gotten used to being single, and he had plenty of interests and activities to fill his time, but these days the house was too quiet and empty at night.

Finding someone—the *right* someone—to share life's adventures would be wonderful.

His parents, still so much in love after sixty years together, had raised him and his older brother to value family. And he did value family. He just enjoyed his work more. Yet that didn't mean he didn't want someone in the wings cheering him on. It sucked when he finished a project and there was no one there to celebrate his success with.

Many of the women he dated over the years had some of the qualities he wanted in a partner. The problem was that none of them had all of Mel's qualities. She was smart, driven, funny, pragmatic, spontaneous—all the things he craved in a mate.

"Anyway, I'm bringing a good friend of mine to the retreat. Her name's Melissa." Brian leaned a hip on the corner of his desk, rotating his neck to ease the tight muscle. "She and I went to college at the University of Texas in Austin, and we clicked the first day we met in class. She's as driven and ambitious as I am. While the rest of the students were drinking, pledging fraternities, and sleeping their way through the coeds, Mel and I were competing for grades. She beat me by this much." He held his thumb and index finger half an inch apart.

"Now I have to meet this superwoman." Marty turned one of Brian's fabric-covered guest chairs around to take a seat. "I've never known anyone to beat you at anything."

Marty looked around Brian's office, nodding at the multitude of plaques and certificates attesting to his achievements. "She must be a hell of a woman to pull one over on you, golden boy. You're the best aerodynamic engineer Daebak has. There's no way Erickson is going to let you transfer without a fight."

"That's why I'm approaching Mr. Shimizu this weekend at the retreat. I *want* this promotion."

I need this promotion.

He remembered Melissa's astonished gasp when he proposed marriage Friday night.

Her instant objection was strategically followed by his logical argument in support of the idea. They were compatible, solid friends, respected each other's career goals, and the big kicker—they weren't getting any younger. For each of her objections, he had a counter argument. He wasn't going to let her win this one. He couldn't.

When she finally, albeit reluctantly, agreed to join him at Silver Fox Resort to "explore the possibility," as she phrased it, Brian wanted to punch the air and do his famous collegiate back flip, then thought better of the idea. He'd probably hurt something. Possibly break his neck.

"Tell me about this super-brain." Marty crossed his arms across the back in the chair he straddled.

A kaleidoscope of images flipped through Brian's mind.

An eighteen-year-old Melissa in blue jeans, a plain red T-shirt, and long blond ponytail, sitting alone in the front row of Mr. Epstein's Physics class. She frowned when he plunked down next to her until he smiled and whispered, "Bet I score higher than you on our first exam."

"Betcha," she said.

They shook hands, and the challenge was on.

And boy, did she challenge him every day to keep his mind alert and his heart in check. His framed photo of Melissa in her black gown and mortarboard, graduating *summa cum laude* with him by her side, was still his favorite. He kept it in the top drawer of his dresser and took it out from time to time to dust off and admire. Even her still image could encourage him to fight on when his projects failed and jobs sucked.

The other photo of Melissa, the one of her in a flight suit, helmet tucked under one arm, a gray, sharp-nosed jet behind her, he kept on his desk at home. She stood ramrod straight, chin up, one hip cocked, confident and strong and beautiful.

The image was in direct contrast to his memory of their visit to her father's grave. She'd worn a simple tank dress that revealed toned arms and legs, and the silky length of her unbound hair hid her face while she knelt in front of the gravestone and traced the engraving with her fingertips. That day was the only time he'd seen her cry. And all these years later, he still remembered the sensation of her wet cheek on his shoulder, his arms circled around her trim waist, firm breasts pressed against his chest, and his heart still in check.

She needed him that day.

Now he needed her.

"Melissa is…" Brian shook his head, trying to find the right words. "Fierce. Fearless. She's the most determined person I've ever met. When she wants something, she makes it happen."

"What does she do?"

"It's classified."

Marty's brow lifted.

"No, seriously. She's in the Air Force, but I'll let her fill you in on the details."

Brian wasn't sure what he could reveal about one of the country's top fighter pilots, even in casual conversation with a trusted friend. "She's flying in Friday morning. Maybe we can meet you and Theresa for lunch. The retreat doesn't officially begin until the cocktail party at five."

"Sounds good. That way Melissa has Theresa to hang out with while you're convincing Mr. Shimizu to give you that job in Austin."

Brian tried to imagine Melissa getting mani/pedis with Theresa and burst out laughing. "Mel doesn't usually have a problem being the odd man out. She got excited when I told her the resort has a complete gym, lap pool, and miles of hiking trails."

"She likes adventure." Marty stroked his chin, eyeing Brian speculatively. "That's an important quality for a man who once sent people into space. What other characteristics might compel a man to up and move halfway across the country?"

Brian shifted uncomfortably.

"Clearly she's intelligent," Marty mused. "She must be loyal, since you've been friends for almost thirty years. Hmm, not sure if she's a practical joker like you, but my guess is no. She's probably the straight man in your double act."

"You're batting a thousand." Brian got up and walked around his desk. "Quit while you're ahead. You'll meet Melissa on Friday, and I guarantee you'll be impressed."

"I can't wait to tell Theresa. She's been nagging me about setting you up. By the way, she didn't think Trish was the right one for you. My wife thinks you need someone exciting in your life who'll get you out of the office more often."

"Yes, but marrying just anyone isn't a good idea either. That's why so many people end up married to the wrong person. They're desperate for love. They don't want to be alone. They want to matter. They want to be the center of someone's world."

"God, that's deep." Marty saluted with two fingers. "Too deep for a Monday morning. I'll catch up with you later."

Perfect timing because Brian's phone vibrated in the back pocket of his khakis. He glanced at the screen to check who was calling and grinned when he saw Melissa's name.

"Morning, BestE."

"Hey, Brian."

There was a hesitation added to her greeting that put him on red alert.

"Am I catching you at a bad time?" she asked.

"No." He strode across the room to close the door, a sinking sensation souring his stomach. "I just got into the office. What's up?"

"I've been thinking about your proposal...er...your proposition."

This was the first awkward conversation they'd had in nearly three decades, as in forever. Brian didn't have a clue how to read the indecision in her voice. Sharp, swift disappointment prickled over his skin.

"No pressure, Mel. Seriously, if you're having second thoughts, it'll just be a weekend between friends. After our call, I upgraded to a two-bedroom villa, just to make sure you'd be comfortable." A knot made the next words hard to choke out. "I really want to see you."

He pressed the phone to his ear as his mouth went dry. *Don't say no. C'mon, you can do this, just don't say no.* He held his breath.

Cancer had almost robbed him of his best friend, and the damn stubborn woman had refused to let him visit while she was undergoing treatment. He endured a year of limited contact, not knowing how she was doing, worrying and wondering and wanting to help, but unable to. She even gave him a hard time when he sent flowers, complaining that she wasn't dead and it wasn't a funeral.

This past year was the first time he resented how strong and independent she was. He wished she knew how to ask for help because he'd drop everything to be there for her.

The thought of losing her was the reality check that made him look at their relationship differently. The threat of not having her in his life forced him to admit how much more he wanted from her. He wanted all of her, for the rest of his life. The problem was that damn friendship line they had drawn so long ago.

"BestE, please don't back out. It'll be fun. You'll see."

"I don't back down from a challenge because of second thoughts. I fly fighter jets, Brian. Remember?" Her droll comments dissolved the lump in his throat.

"Is that how you see this?" he asked. "As a challenge?"

"Well…yes." There it was, her practical side. She was still nervous, he could tell. "I'm worried what will happen to our friendship if this crazy idea of yours doesn't work out. Marriage is a big step. I'm not the kind of woman to enter into a legal and emotional commitment like this lightly."

"That's one of the reasons *this* marriage makes perfect sense. Neither of us is a quitter. We respect each other and get along. Hell, we even communicate well, this call being a case in point."

"I don't know how to be more than friends. I woke up this morning and my first thought was, 'I can't wait to see MechE on Friday,' but then I panicked. Are we supposed to kiss? Hold hands? Sleep together?"

His heart expanded when he recognized Melissa's unspoken plea for reassurance. He could deal with uncertainty. What he couldn't deal with was *No way, Jose.*

"We'll figure it out together, Mel. We always have." A memory made him chuckle. "Remember the Cauchy theory problem Mr. Hines challenged us to solve on the first day of variables class?"

"Yah, I tried to solve the equation all semester and then realized he'd written the base problem wrong and challenged him on it. The problem was unsolvable as written."

"Exactly." He drew a confident breath. "But you worked and worked at solving the problem until you knew it couldn't be answered, just like the way you trained and practiced to be a fighter pilot. It didn't happen overnight."

"Are you saying this relationship is going to be a math problem that needs to be solved?" She snickered. "That's the most ridiculous thing I've ever heard. It's a good thing you work for a car manufacturer and not a greeting card company."

"No." He managed a chuckle. "I'm saying it's going to take time, but we'll work it out in the end."

Silence stretched into a long pause, and he worried that if he said one more thing, it might push the conversation into the danger zone.

"I can't laugh about that. You may be right." She snickered again, and this time the tone was softer and more serious.

"Keep your eye on the target, General Davenport. You've got your assignment and the necessary resources to accomplish it. Report for duty on Friday at 0900 hours."

"Yes, sir," she said, sounding like a big-eyed, ambitious new recruit, then disconnected.

I can't wait to see you. He rubbed his thumb over the screen where Melissa's name and number had appeared.

Friday couldn't get here soon enough.

Chapter 3

The gentle bump announced that Melissa was safely on the ground, where she continued to navigate down the regional airport runway and communicate with the tower.

The flight from Stinson Municipal Airport out of San Antonio, where she stored her pride and joy, a 2002 Beechcraft A36 Bonanza, had been smooth as silk with clear weather shaving a few minutes off the three-hour, eight-minute trip.

And like always, being in the air, looking down at the earth from above, made her practically burst with pure joy. There was a piece of her that only came alive when she was floating on air.

After confirming arrangements—refueling and overnight ramp parking until late Sunday evening—Melissa grabbed her carry-on. She strode across the tarmac, scanning the small terminal building's windows for a glimpse of Brian.

Her gut churned from eighty percent nervous excitement and twenty percent trepidation. Facing Brian within the new parameters was going to be tricky. This new slant to their relationship was making her nervous about how to navigate. She hoped once they confronted the new boundaries in person they'd settle into their usual easy camaraderie.

She shaded her eyes against the glare of the midmorning sun, grateful for the warmth of her jacket. Central California was a few degrees cooler than Texas this time of year, and she knew the weather at the resort would be even chillier, since it sat on the coast.

In fact, she couldn't wait to check in to the Silver Fox Resort for some self-care. It had been a long time since she had someone to talk to who wasn't military. The anticipation alone had lifted her mood.

"Mel!"

She whipped around to the right and spotted the silhouette of a tall, lean man. Even in the shadow of the terminal's overhang, she recognized the set of his shoulders and the lazy runner's lope that carried him closer while the sun glinted off his short gray hair and mirrored sunglasses.

Her heart sped up to keep pace with her stride.

Brian didn't bother with an awkward pause like the one that slowed her steps at the last minute. He caught her up in his arms, forcing her to drop her suitcase as he twirled her around. After a few dizzying spins, he set her back down and curled his hands over her shoulders, standing back to examine her from head to toe.

"You look great. If I didn't know better, I'd never guess you've been battling cancer for the past year. As much as I liked your hair long, you are absolutely rocking that short cut."

Relief shone bright in his blue-gray eyes, and for the first time, Melissa realized she hadn't been the only person affected by the frightening diagnosis.

Her mother didn't seem to care—or care much, anyway—and hadn't cared for a long time.

To her shock and dismay, her mom remarried less than a year after her father's death, and she and Paul moved to Palm Beach while Melissa was still in college. Somehow over the years her once-close relationship with her mother dwindled down to barely a flicker, until the flowers and cards wishing her well while she struggled with cancer seemed like an insult.

From that moment on, stubbornness and disappointment wouldn't allow her to accept help. If her retired mother couldn't spare a couple of weeks to help, who could? She'd handle the situation. Just like the other times life kicked her in the teeth.

"I'm fine." Her smile felt artificial, stretching her skin and pulling her mouth tight. The doctor said the odds of the cancer returning were low, but he couldn't guarantee a future free from the threat.

Most of the time Melissa ignored the risk, but with Brian looking at her with his heart in his eyes, she knew she'd have to lay it out for him.

It was one of the reasons—okay, the main reason— holding her back from jumping into marriage with her whole heart and soul. She and Brian had made it through life this far without a spouse and done all right. What if she accepted his proposal, allowed him to fall in love with her, and then had another go-round with cancer? The next time might not end so well. Was that fair to him?

It was a decision she'd have to allow him to make...but not today.

She'd promised herself the weekend. Two and a half days to test the waters. Two nights to reveal parts of herself she'd never shared with a man. She trembled at the thought, so she bent to retrieve her suitcase.

"I've got it." Brian leaned down and grabbed the handle before she could move. "How was your flight?" He glanced back at her pride and joy. "I'm hoping one of these days you'll give me a ride." She started to turn, but he grabbed her hand, twining their fingers together. "We can't now. I'm parked this way. It's an hour-plus drive to the resort, and I promised a friend we'd meet for lunch. But if you're hungry how, we can stop and pick up something light."

Brian had always been a chatterbox, and she loved how his light banter filled the gaps stretched taut by her anxiety about this new arrangement. The tension weighing down her limbs eased, making her feel lighter, more lithe, more alive with energy.

She let out a breath even she hadn't known she was holding. "I had juice and a nut bar over Arizona. I can wait."

With her hand in Brian's, she crossed the jam-packed parking lot. Brian slowed periodically to greet a traveler, nodding and smiling and yakking away the entire time.

"So, tell me." She tugged on his arm to get his attention. "Why is this thing we're going to such a big deal? You seem nervous. That's not like you."

"Daebak, my company, is the leading car manufacturer in Japan. And sales are increasing in the US, thanks to their accelerated development of vehicles that use sustainable energy. The top guys are coming in to chat with the US leadership team." He clicked the remote, and the trunk on a sleek silver sedan popped open. Brian ran a hand lovingly over the curved line of the quarter panel. "This is the model I helped design."

"Impressive."

He chuckled. "You'd say the same thing if I drove up in a Ford Fiesta."

This guy knew her too well. Melissa could rattle off the specs on jets and prop jobs, but cars were just a way to get from one place to another. If the equipment wasn't exceeding the speed of sound, she paid little attention.

Brian stowed her luggage, closed the trunk, then settled his hand in the small of her back, escorting her to the passenger door. "You're the copilot this time."

She twisted away, leaning against the door, meeting Brian's steady gaze. "Thanks for inviting me."

She searched his eyes, wanting to understand why he invited her. If she spotted even one ounce of sympathy, he'd get a tongue-lashing, but what she saw, the soft longing, surprised her and heated her core.

He rested the heel of one hand on the roof of the car, closing the space between them. "Thanks for coming."

He was going to kiss her.

Not a friendly peck like they'd shared in the past, but a real kiss. The kind a man and woman share when they're attracted to one another, when they have feelings for each other.

When they're falling in love…

Her lids fluttered shut, her lips parted, and her chin lifted. Waiting…

"I was saving this for the resort, but it feels like this might be the right time." Brian's whisper was followed by the brush of his mouth across hers. "Open your eyes, Mel."

He pulled something out of a pocket and leaned away so he could present his hand, palm up, a red velvet box cradled in his elegant fingers.

"I know it may be a bit premature, but I want you to know I'm serious." He gestured to the box with his chin.

Fingers trembling, heart pumping like she'd ejected from a jet headed toward a mountain, she took the box. Opening the hinged lid, she stared at the thin, diamond-studded band next to the matching silicone ring. He'd done his homework. He'd kept the bands military simple. It was the ring she would have chosen for herself—nothing fancy, but oh, so beautiful.

"Am I supposed to wear this now?" Her attention zipped between the ring and his face.

"Try it on." Brian took the box and carefully wiggled the rings out of their white satin bed. "Left hand, please."

Complying, Melissa offered her ring finger, the surreal moment leaving her dizzy and dazed.

The sister-rings fit perfectly.

She examined the band and stones, gleaming richly against her short, unpolished nails and unadorned fingers. The implications of accepting the ring, of *maybe* really accepting Brian's proposal, stole her breath.

How could they make a long-distance marriage work? It was almost guaranteed that the Air Force would relocate her from Texas. She could land anywhere. Brian's job tied him to California. He'd worked his entire life for a job with a company like Daebak.

On the first of December, she and Brian would turn fifty. That half-century mark meant they were set in their ways. Too old for children, in her opinion. Too young for front porch rocking chairs. What would a life together look like? What would it mean for her career? His? They'd poured everything into achieving their respective professional goals. Now what?

And were those achievements worth the risk if their marriage failed?

"I have the same questions and doubts running through my mind, too." Brian, who knew her so well they didn't need words, rested his forehead against hers, then nuzzled his nose into her hair and inhaled. "Neither of us is the type to run away from something because it might be hard or other people say it can't be done. Let's give you and me a try."

"Trying and doing are two different things, Brian. When you try, you hope. When you do, you succeed." She circled her arms around Brian's waist, listening to his heartbeat beneath her cheek. It felt good. Right. Like she belonged here.

Not caring that they had a long drive along the beautiful California coast or that Brian's coworkers were gathering for an executive retreat, Melissa leaned into his strength.

Finally, for the first time since her dad's death, she had someone to lean on.

A cool breeze teased the ends of her hair, and the sibilant burr of traffic sounded from a nearby freeway. Birds chirped, and airplane engines whined and then bellowed. Brian smelled of soap, minty toothpaste, coffee, and clean cotton, and the smells saturated her dry, cracked heart.

When it finally settled into a normal rhythm again, she dropped her arms. Brian waited expectantly.

"Let's do this." She rose up on her tiptoes and kissed him like she wanted this engagement to work more than she wanted anything else in life.

Silver Fox Resort and Spa was stunning, sitting on more than four hundred acres of the Northern California coastline.

In addition to the main building, private villas, and retreat facilities, there was a stable, a vineyard, and an assortment of other amenities offering guests a tranquil escape. The rolling hills, rocky cliffs, and endless expanse of blue ocean were highlights of the natural beauty of the location, but inside the resort it was pure luxury.

After a quick shower at their private sea-view villa and a change into slacks and a white linen blouse, Melissa hurried up the path to the main lobby. Brian had already changed and said he'd meet her at the restaurant off the lobby.

She waved to Zoey Foster, the resort owner who checked them in, and slowed long enough to appreciate the wood beams crisscrossing the white plaster ceiling, the large rock fireplace in which a fire crackled merrily against the bracing November chill, and the inviting banks of seating around redwood coffee tables. The perfume of fresh flowers and sugared vanilla scented the air along with woodsmoke and leather.

The sight of Brian waiting for her at the entrance to the restaurant hurried her along.

She ogled his trim body and appreciated how much work it took to maintain the body of a man ten years younger.

When she kissed him earlier, her hands had curved over his pecs, sliding down to a toned abdomen that made her hungry to touch bare skin instead of starched fabric. He let her control the kiss, seeming to sense that the engagement ring took things from zero to Mach 2, maybe a bit too fast for a trial engagement. They'd both been breathless when she finally pulled away, wanting more but not ready for more.

Brian's entire being lit up when he saw her. One corner of his mouth tilted up, pulling her eyes to the scar in the middle of his chin. He was so familiar, so dear, yet everything seemed new and different.

Slinging an arm around her shoulders, he bent to press his lips against her temple. "Marty and Theresa just got here," he whispered close to her ear. "I sent them to the table and asked them to order a round of appetizers. I'm famished."

Nerves fluttered in her belly, warring with hunger, but Melissa took a reassuring breath. She'd never met any of Brian's California friends or coworkers, and here she was, temporarily engaged until they decided if it made sense to move forward with his suggestion that they marry.

A server in black with a signature resort apron guided them through the spacious dining room to a four-top next to a window overlooking the California coastline. A large bird flew alone across the seascape, which made a perfect backdrop for the afternoon meal.

A pudgy man with dark-framed glasses, close-cropped brown hair edged with gray, and expressive eyes stood as they approached the table. His wife, a slender brunette with shoulder-length curly brown hair, wide, round eyes, and not a brush of makeup except lip gloss, remained seated but smiled in welcome.

"Hello. You must be Melissa." The man held out a hand and shook hers once with a soft pump. "I'm Marty Rosenblatt, and this is my wife, Theresa."

The woman's eyes locked onto the double bands on her left hand, then moved to Melissa's face, to Brian's, and then back. Her brows dipped briefly in curiosity, but she didn't ask the question waiting to be answered.

"We've been looking forward to meeting you." Theresa scooted her chair a fraction of an inch left to allow Brian to settle in the seat next to her. That put Melissa across the table from her. "Brian said the two of you go back to college days."

Marty offered her the breadbasket filled with fresh-from-the-oven rolls sprinkled with poppy seeds. The aroma alone made her drool, but she managed to contain her urges and waved the basket away. "We ordered the bacon and goat cheese-stuffed mushrooms and whipped feta. The menu describes the dish as being drizzled with honey from the beehives nurtured right here at the resort. Theresa already bought two jars of the stuff from the gift shop."

"This will probably be our only visit to the resort, so I'm going to splurge." Theresa selected one of the rolls and set it daintily on her bread plate. "I'm taking home plenty of souvenirs to replicate the experience—as much as I can in a house packed with four kids, a dog, two cats, and a hamster."

"That sounds like a handful." Uncertainty dampened Melissa's pleasure. The conversation was taking her into uncharted territory. Would all the spouses be talking about raising babies and kids? She knew nothing about either. "It must keep you busy."

Her new duties as the Air Force Recruiting Service Center commander required some entertaining and hostess duties, and she could hold her own in a room full of brass. Exchanging small talk about children and domestic matters was like listening to a group of people speaking a foreign language. She could pick up bits and pieces but understanding the intricacies? Not so much.

"Don't let her fool you. She's a flawless master of the house." Marty's chest puffed up with pride. "It's her book publishing business and a dozen other do-gooder projects that chew up the time."

"What do you write?" Melissa relaxed, leaning back in her chair, genuinely intrigued.

"I write children's books. My latest release is *The Adventures of Timmy the Toad and his Animal Friends*."

A surge of admiration forced Melissa to re-examine her initial impression of this obviously capable woman. "I can't say I've read your book." Melissa smiled and took a sip from her water glass. "What else do you do?"

As Theresa revealed details about her and Marty's busy life, Melissa watched Brian and Marty in her peripheral vision while the two men talked sports.

A few minutes later, a polite waiter interrupted the conversation. "May I share the day's specials with you?"

The group nodded in unison.

"Chef Nate's Special of the Day starts off with an endive salad with pecan-encrusted goat cheese. The main course is Dijon-and-herb-crusted salmon served on a bed of arugula with homemade dill vinaigrette, followed by banana bread pudding with a caramel rum sauce for dessert."

"Oh, that sounds delicious." Theresa's eyes flared with excitement. "I'll have that."

Melissa ordered the same, minus dessert, while Marty went with the blue cheese Kobe burger and Brian selected the lobster macaroni and cheese with a wedge salad.

They opted for bottled water with lemon wedges, which relieved Melissa since she felt the need for hydration.

"It's a good thing we're eating lunch early." Marty speared one of the mushrooms a server had delivered while they ordered. "The cocktail party includes light appetizers, but Janelle from the C-Suite said management is going all out since the VIPs will be here. Prime rib, caviar and crème fraiche, tuna ceviche. The chef here is award-winning and will be making his signature Dulce de Leche Cheesecake for the group." Marty pointed a thumb at his wife. "Theresa already checked out the menu."

Theresa nibbled on a dab of whipped butter on the corner of her roll and groaned. "I'm going to gain twenty pounds in two days."

"Gain thirty." Marty patted his wife's arm. "I'll still love you. Most of all, I want you to enjoy yourself this weekend."

Melissa caught Brian watching her. He gave a tiny shrug and winked. She swallowed to keep from laughing.

She couldn't imagine Brian acting all lovey-dovey like Marty, but what did she know about old married couples? The whole long-term relationship concept was new because most of the military couples she knew had either been divorced and remarried multiple times or kept their private lives…private.

Sure, she had her military family, and she wouldn't give them up for anything, but the thought of having someone share her pot of coffee in the morning was just weird.

What she did know was that she liked this sense of belonging, being part of the circle of friends Brian had assembled for himself in California. He'd always been as ambitious and competitive as she was, but her approach was to buckle down and do it herself, not allowing others to distract her. Brian, on the other hand, was a true extrovert. He thrived on group synergy and collaboration.

Strange how they were so different, yet so alike.

"Brian mentioned you two share a birthday." Marty poured the last of the bottled water and looked around for the waiter to ask for more.

"December first." Melissa folded her hands and rested them in her lap.

"Same year and everything," Brian added. "I'm older, though. Born two hours and fifty-four minutes before she made her grand…um…entrance."

Brian glanced toward the restaurant's entrance.

Marty gave a low whistle.

A trio of Japanese businessmen was being led to a window-view table one over from theirs. The three men looked to be in their sixties, wore dark suits, muted ties, and short, neatly groomed hair. They carried themselves with formal precision, in contrast to the informality creeping into US business etiquette, which Melissa considered neither good nor bad.

"Mr. Shimizu and company," Marty intoned.

"Who are they?" Theresa mimicked her husband's stage whisper.

"Bigwigs from Tokyo headquarters." Brian's jaw muscle rippled briefly.

Melissa's attention darted between Brian and the VIPs, her senses on high alert. She was missing something, but what? The gentlemen stopped at their assigned table but turned in their direction.

A short, slender man with thick white hair, rimless glasses, and a classic gray pinstriped suit led the trio their way, stopping at their table.

He bent at the waist. "*Konnichiwa*, Misters Newbury and Rosenblatt." He straightened and signaled to the other two men. "It is my pleasure to introduce my associates, Mr. Ito and Mr. Yamamoto."

Brian and Marty stood, the five men exchanging handshakes.

"This is my wife, Theresa Rosenblatt." Marty stood behind Theresa, who smiled and nodded.

Brian moved closer and rested a hand on Melissa's shoulder, his fingers tighter than was comfortable.

"Sirs, this is Melissa Davenport. My fiancée."

Chapter 4

*B*rian knew he was in trouble the moment Melissa stiffened. From that moment on, lunch was pleasant, but tense. Melissa had a good enough game face that he doubted Marty or Theresa picked up any negativity.

He sure had. And now the wall of pretense was about to come crashing down.

Her hands clenched and released as she paced back and forth across the villa's tan carpet. The small seating area with a couch, table for two, and a beverage area with mini-fridge wasn't very large, so every half-dozen steps Melissa swiveled and headed back his way.

"I can't believe you announced our engagement in front of everyone." She turned, planted her hands on her hips, and glared, "We are *not* officially engaged, and you stated it like our engagement was a done deal."

He held out his hands in front of him. "Mel, I was wrong. It was an error in judgment," he offered, knowing he deserved her fury. "I'm sorry."

"Why would you blurt it out like that? This"—she threw

her hands in the air—"this was supposed to be a trial run. We haven't even decided if this is real or not."

She hadn't decided.

He already had.

Looking back, Brian realized he made his decision back when she revealed her breast cancer diagnosis. Life didn't come with guarantees. Twelve months and another failed relationship made him wake up to the fact he didn't want to live alone anymore, and Mel was the right woman for him.

"Theresa noticed your ring at lunch, and I didn't want people speculating."

"They shouldn't be speculating about me—you, maybe, but not me. I'm sure Marty isn't the only coworker who knows you're a serial dater. This is a disaster. If this gets out…I should never have agreed to this."

"Mel, calm down."

"'Calm down,' he says. No, I will *not* calm down. You told everyone we're engaged." She stomped her foot for emphasis. "Engaged!" She pointed at him. "You need to fix this, now!"

Brian felt his own ire rising. "Sit down. Please. Let's talk about this."

She raked him with another look sharp enough to peel the flesh off his bones, but she sat. But he could still feel the darts of anger being thrown at him. "We agreed this weekend was temporary. A chance to try on the idea of a committed, romantic relationship. I'm not ready to send out wedding announcements, Brian. Not even close."

"Again, I'm sorry. Truly sorry." He moved around the end of the couch. "But being in a relationship doesn't mean hiding behind closed doors. I need help understanding why you're so angry. Are you uncomfortable with the idea of marriage? Or the idea of marriage to me?"

Her eyes flared wide, and her shoulders dropped from their tight, defensive hunch. "What kind of question is that?"

"You came here so we could test-drive a new model for our relationship." He lowered to the couch and clasped his hands between his knees, already discouraged, and they weren't even half a day into their temporary engagement. "You accept my ring, kiss me, then flip out when I casually mention you're my fiancée."

"'Casually mention?'" She cocked a brow in disbelief. "You practically announced it to the entire restaurant."

She was right. He was sorry, truly, and accepted it was a jerk kind of thing to do, but it was sort of funny.

She caught the twitch of his lip, lifted both brows and stared him down. "This better not be one of your practical jokes. Because if it is, I'm warning you, paybacks are going to be severe."

"This is no joke, and it's definitely not as funny as the time we tried to find out how many plastic cups we could shove into Professor Cappelli's VW Bug. That was a classic."

Ah, there it was. The slight pucker that revealed Melissa was holding back a smile. "I'd say it's more on par with the time we all wore fake mustaches into Professor Streeck's final exams. He was so proud of his mustache, and he was a good sport about our joke." She softened a bit more, angling her knees toward his.

"Mel, I really am sorry. I don't know what compelled me to introduce you as my fiancée. I know how private you are. It was poor timing. The wrong place. Private information, not for public consumption." He wove his fingers together, thumbs circling as he considered his actions. "I really want this...us...to work, and I've been figuring out the logistics. I'm an engineer. I design and test complicated prototypes. Unfortunately, there's no design manual for marriage. No instruction guide that says insert Tab A into Slot B."

Her lips pressed together before she tilted her head back

and loosed a belly laugh that released the tension piling up between them like row after row of concrete blocks.

"Bri, dude, there is a guide for that. It's called the Kama Sutra."

"That wasn't on any of the college syllabi."

"Maybe you need remedial lessons."

"Are you volunteering to be my study partner?" He moved in closer, and she didn't back away this time. An encouraging sign. "You feel it, too, don't you?" He took her hand in his to feel the pulse point at her wrist.

Melissa still didn't say anything, but she had leaned in a bit closer.

"Does that make you uncomfortable? Being attracted to me, knowing I'm attracted to you?"

She shook her head, her top two teeth worrying her lower lip until it was crimson and swollen.

"How long has it been since you slept with a man?"

"Lee Soderbeck."

"Lee Soder— my god, Mel. You dated him briefly our junior year."

"I've been focused on other things, Brian." She didn't meet his eyes. "And once I joined the Air Force, it was hard to meet anyone who wasn't military, and you know I made a pledge I would never marry a military guy. Plus, I want to keep my private and professional worlds separate."

"I won't wreck your reputation or your career." He brushed his knuckles over her cheek, following the line of her jaw, and trailing a finger down her neck.

"One of us will have to forfeit our career if we want this marriage to work. Long-distance relationships have notoriously poor outcomes."

Her words, though true, were ruining the moment, and he refused to let her call it quits before they even got started.

"Cart before the horse, Mel. The goal this weekend is to explore the potential. At least give us these few days."

Slanting his head, he leaned close and tasted her with the tip of his tongue. Her lips parted, her breath warming his chin as he deepened his exploration. He nibbled her lower lip playfully until he felt her smile and knew he had imprinted her flavor, her essence, on his memory and his heart.

His muscles clenched as he resisted the urge to push Melissa further. Instead, he nipped tiny kisses along the sensitive area behind her ear.

"I think there's plenty of potential here," she admitted before pulling away.

"We're negotiating new boundaries, Mel. It's important we communicate. We have to be able to talk about anything, even topics that make us uncomfortable."

"That's never been a problem for us." She got to her feet and straightened her shirt.

He rose, waiting for her to make eye contact. "We've never been more than just friends. With that came boundaries. Now we need to make new ones."

"Husband and wife." Her sigh came from the soles of her feet. "You have more experience dating than I have."

"I'm not sure I'd call this dating." He jammed his hands in his pockets. "Dating is when people go out, spend time together on a regular basis. Sometimes it remains casual; sometimes it turns into something serious. This is…more than dating."

"Call it what you want. You still have far, far more experience than I do."

"It's not about experience. It's about being real with each other." Brian pulled his bestie into a hug. "Come on. Let's go check out the rest of the resort, maybe take a walk on the beach. We have plenty of time before the cocktail party, and I want you to line up some activities for while I'm in meetings tomorrow."

Melissa wrapped him in a hug, "I'm sorry for getting angry. It's just this is all so new. I feel out of control."

He squeezed her tight. "It's okay. I've got you. You're safe." He let her go reluctantly.

"If we're going for a walk, I want to put on different shoes." She padded into her bedroom.

Brian watched her go, admiring the seductive sway of her hips.

To think this beautiful, talented, accomplished woman had been right in front of him for nearly thirty years.

Enough time wasted.

By Sunday night he needed to convince Melissa to say yes. For real.

Forever.

$\mathcal{M}$elissa hooked her arm through Brian's, proud to be entering the cocktail party with the most handsome man at the resort. Definitely the hottest, kindest, most thoughtful man in her world.

The navy sport coat emphasized the breadth of his shoulders and muscular back, while the tailored trousers hugged his lean hips. He wore a light blue shirt with a fuchsia and lavender tie and matching pocket square. The pop of color suited his playful personality.

They hadn't intentionally coordinated their wardrobes, but her dress was a slight shade darker than Brian's suit. The sleeveless sheath fit as if tailored for her athletic frame, the nipped-in waist flattering her modest bustline and the flare of her hips. She was still self-conscious about her short, cropped hair, compliments of her chemo treatments, but Brian's low whistle of appreciation reassured her the simple pixie cut almost looked natural.

And when he kissed her bare nape, making her shiver, her nerves scattered to the four winds.

The only jewelry she wore was Brian's engagement ring

and the half-carat diamond studs her mother gave her when she graduated from high school. The earrings meant as much as the ring, maybe more, because it turned out that her father chose them for her just weeks before his tragic death.

"Nervous?" Brian covered the hand resting on his forearm with his own as they strolled down a well-maintained garden path to the building where the retreat meetings would be held.

The sun, a huge orange globe, was just starting to sink into the ocean, dropping the temperature enough that Melissa tugged her cashmere wrap tighter around her.

"No. I've attended my share of corporate mixers. Your dress code, of course, is different from mine, but these functions are all the same." She squeezed his arm playfully. "Now that everyone knows we're engaged, there are no more secrets to worry about being revealed."

His fingers flexed over hers for a second, and she peered at him.

"Are *you* nervous?" She bumped her hip against his. "You seemed flustered when Mr. Shimizu said hello at lunch."

"I have a proposal to discuss with Mr. Shimizu before the weekend is out. I've met him a few times before today, but approaching him means going around my boss, and it's a risky move. If my boss finds out…"

"That's a no-no in my profession. Everything goes up the chain of command."

"That's how it usually works in the civilian world, but I have a sneaking suspicion Erickson would kill my idea. It's something I think will be better for me…for us…long-term."

"Whatever you have to talk to Mr. Shimizu about sounds important."

"It is."

Brian seemed disinclined to elaborate, so she dropped the topic. Living in a world where most subjects were classified had ingrained discretion into her life's standard operating procedure.

Instead, she absorbed the bronzing effect of the setting sun, bands of clouds colored violet, magenta, and crimson, spindly trees dotting the rugged hillsides. She inhaled a mix of salty ocean and tangy pine.

"It's peaceful here." She nestled a bit closer to Brian's warmth. "The rumble of the ocean is soothing, but I miss the sounds of jets."

Brian treated her to one of his special husky laughs. They crested a small knoll, the path continuing on to the clearing where the retreat building awaited them. Lights twinkled inside and out, creating a festive atmosphere, and laughter and music radiated from the building, revealing the cocktail party had already started.

"Are we late?" Melissa quickened her pace.

"Relax. We're on California time, not military time. People will stroll in for the first hour. After that you're considered late."

Like the rest of the resort, the retreat lodge was a combination of rustic charm and sumptuous luxury. The bamboo plank flooring was polished to a glossy sheen that contrasted with the dark walls and wooden ceiling beams. Glass-paned windows looked out onto the grounds and the hazy purple twilight. Tables and chairs were set up in groups of four and eight, while food stations occupied each corner of the long, rectangular meeting room, and a bar draped with white cloth stood just outside the double doors leading into the main area.

Men and women wearing cocktail attire milled around the room, the clusters shifting and morphing like the plasma in a lava lamp. Several individuals cast inquisitive looks in their direction, which Melissa ignored. These were Brian's associates. He could handle their curiosity.

Theresa waved, beckoning for Melissa and Brian to join her and Marty.

"What an attractive couple you make," Theresa cooed.

She wore a coral chiffon dress with a turquoise paisley pattern on top that brought out the reddish highlights in her dark hair and played off her pale, creamy complexion.

"You look more like a fashion model than a fighter pilot." Marty shoveled a scoop of tiny caviar beads into his mouth, brushing stray crumbs off the lapels of his tweed suitcoat.

Theresa rolled her eyes. "What my husband means is, you look lovely. I was fascinated to hear about your career and accomplishments during lunch. So many people—us included, I'm afraid—assume our military pilots are men. I had no idea how many women are defending our nation from the cockpit."

Melissa shifted, uncomfortable with Theresa's admiration. She didn't fly jets to make a social or political statement. Her father was a Naval aviator. The earliest pictures of her were of her dad in his flight uniform and her cradled in his arm or on his shoulders in front of whichever plane had been assigned to him at the time. Their bond solidified her career resolve early.

People often fixated on the fact that she was a general and fighter pilot. While both were her greatest achievements to date, the positions didn't define her as a woman, or her life beyond.

Or did they?

The realization slammed into her like a gut punch. She wanted to deny the truth, argue, refute the claim...but she was the sum of her title of general. Her career, flying, being promoted to the next rank, moving from one duty station to another—that was her life.

Brian saw past her rank and medals. He made her feel like more and made her want more.

He touched her elbow, pulling her out of her thoughts. "What can I get you from the bar?"

"Wine. Red, please."

"Be right back."

She watched him maneuver through the crowd, greeting colleagues, pausing to chat, clapping men on the back, being introduced to spouses. Brian had something special, a charisma that drew people to him. He liked being around people, connected easily…yet he'd never managed to settle down, and she wondered why that was. And what drove him to want something more permanent now? Something lasting, with her. Was it just because they were friends and had made a silly vow on their graduation night? Or was it more?

Her answer to that question was yes. She wanted more.

Brian's motives remained unclear, but part of her mission this weekend was to uncover the truth.

"Hi, Marty, ladies. Are you enjoying the party?" A dark-haired man with the look of a high school jock gone soft joined their trio. His gaze jumped from her legs to her breasts to the ring on her left hand.

"We haven't met." He stretched out his hand expectantly. "I'm Greg Erickson."

"Melissa Davenport." His hand was sweaty, and he held on for several seconds too long.

"I understand you're a fighter pilot with the US Air Force. Should I call you sergeant or admiral?" he snickered.

"The Air Force doesn't have admirals. That's the Navy and Coast Guard. Sergeant is an enlisted rank for Marines, Air Force, and Army personnel. Neither are correct." She refused to give the scuzzball the correct titles or relieve any uncomfortable tension he might feel. He should have done his homework.

"There's a rumor going around that congratulations are

in order." Greg waggled his thick brows. "Will that make you Mrs. Sergeant Newburg?"

She took an instant dislike to this man because of his disrespect for the title she earned—and retained—through hard work and perseverance, and for his sarcasm. This was the boss Brian feared would nix his proposal, the man forcing Brian to go around him for a fair shake. No wonder he didn't trust this guy.

"Marty," she said a bit louder than she might have otherwise, "would you recommend the prime rib or caviar?" Angling her back toward Greg Erickson, Melissa slipped her tongue between her teeth to keep from saying something that might cause trouble for Brian.

Marty took her cue. "Start with the caviar. In fact, I'm ready for seconds. Would you care to join me?"

"If you will please excuse us." She turned back toward Greg.

"Nice to meet you, Sergeant. Have fun this weekend."

With every step toward the food tables her temper flared higher. "Is he always such a jerk?" she asked Marty while Theresa peeked over her shoulder, back at Greg, as they moved away.

"He's not usually so blatant about it." Marty made a sound as if he just realized something. "He may have had one too many drinks, but I think he's jealous of Brian. He only got the promotion after Brian turned the offer down. Brian wanted to finish working on the project he was on or he might have considered the job."

"That's not an excuse for Greg's behavior." Theresa took a small white plate from a table holding utensils, napkins, and china, then got in line at the caviar station. "Especially to the guest of an employee."

"I'll report the incident to HR on Monday." Marty waited with them but didn't take a plate for himself.

"Please talk to Brian about this before you go to HR. I don't want there to be any repercussions for him, and Greg seems like the vindictive type." Melissa ignored the acid churning in her stomach.

Greg Erickson wasn't the first condescending male chauvinist she'd dealt with. Plenty of men, including some she served with, believed women belonged in the kitchen, not the cockpit. Letting their bad behavior slide didn't benefit anyone but confronting ignorant bullies like Erickson still made her palms sweat and nerves flutter.

"I can ignore what happened, but I think you and Brian should decide together how best to handle this," she said.

"Are you okay?" Theresa filled the gap between Marty and her, concern etching a line between her brows.

"I'm fine. I've learned not to give my power away to men like Greg Erickson." She'd moved to the front of the line and added a dollop of shiny reddish-orange ikura—salmon roe— to her plate, although she'd lost her appetite.

"There you are." Brian held a glass of red wine in each hand, oblivious to what had happened. "Marty, can you find us somewhere to sit?"

"Sure. I saw some empty tables near the fireplace."

"Brian, I got enough for us both. Would you like anything else?"

He peered over her shoulder. "Looks good to me," he said, but he wasn't looking at her plate.

And just like that, her mood lightened. "I was talking about food."

"I was thinking about what I wanted to nibble."

"We need to go sit down, now." She moved away from the table. "Before you make a spectacle of yourself."

Once settled at the table, Melissa fortified herself with a hearty sip of wine while Theresa and Marty went off in pursuit of more delicacies.

"Mel?" he asked in a manner that asked a more important question. He knew she was upset. He stood with both hands on the back of his empty seat, searching her face.

"I'm fine. Really."

He nodded his acceptance of her explanation, but the look in his eye said they would talk about it later. "I'm going for some prime rib. Can I get you anything?"

"I'll start with this." She indicated the plate of caviar, crème fraiche, and toast points.

"Ah, Mr. Newburg and Ms. Davenport." Mr. Shimizu, looking quite dapper in a black suit, appeared beside their table and inclined his head in greeting. "I hoped for a private moment such as this. I have become aware, Mr. Newburg, you are interested in being considered for the Global Environmental Program Vice President position at our plant in Austin."

Brian paled, his eyes shifting nervously toward Melissa. "Yes, I…ah…would be open to the possibility, sir."

"I'm sorry to disappoint you, but the position has already been filled." The older Japanese man offered a sympathetic smile. "However, there are many opportunities within Daebak for a talented individual such as yourself. We have new programs in development that would benefit from your unique knowledge and experience. The Personnel Office is aware of your desires and will be in contact with you as the positions become available."

"Thank you, Mr. Shimizu. I appreciate your consideration."

The CEO nodded and took his leave, wandering back through the crowd.

Melissa's ears rang, drowning out the rest of the conversation. She stared at Brian, shock and betrayal turning her lungs into a blast furnace, making it impossible to breathe. He was already making plans to relocate to Texas.

Wow. And she thought the surprises were over with.

"What's going on here, Brian?"

"I was hoping to put in a transfer so we could be closer. In case…"

"In case what?" She watched him blink several times as he tried to come up with something to say.

"Look." Brian shifted his weight and leaned in. "Austin is much closer to San Antonio than San Francisco, and if something were to happen, I want to be closer to you."

"You mean closer to help me if I get sick again." Her cheeks heated with a combination of frustration and fury. "So, this sudden engagement really isn't about us being together; it's about you wanting to take care of me if the cancer comes back."

"Well, yeah. That's partly the reason. The other reason was to take a lateral move, possibly get a promotion."

But instinct told her the last part was just an excuse. The cancer pity party was more likely his main reason for pursuing the transfer.

Maybe she was being naive, trusting in the existence of soul mates and happily-ever-afters instead of realizing relationships at fifty came with a lot of extra baggage stuffed with junk. Junk she didn't want to deal with.

The bitter tang of regret overpowered the oak-and-blackberry taste of her wine.

Her stomach revolted against the onslaught of emotions. She should have laughed off Brian's suggestion that they marry just because of a drunken promise made all those years and years ago. Coming out to California was a huge mistake.

She rose from the chair, brushing aside Brian's hand. She needed air. She needed space. She needed…she no longer knew what she needed.

Tears burned the backs of her eyes, but she would not

allow them to form. She blinked them away, ignoring Theresa calling her name and Greg Erickson smirking as he tossed back the amber liquid in his drink glass.

She'd forgotten her wrap in her haste to leave the lodge. Shivering with cold and the fear that her friendship with Brian had been irrevocably damaged, she sought the privacy of the moonless night.

Chapter 6

"*L*et her go." Theresa Rosenblatt clutched the sleeve of Brian's jacket, holding him in place.

Brian's impulse was to shake off Theresa's hand and go after Melissa, but something in her voice stopped him.

"Give her a little time and space." Theresa spoke to him only, then in a louder voice, advised Marty they were going to get a breath of fresh air and that they would be back in a few minutes.

Brian noticed the look Theresa and Marty exchanged. He envied their bond, wanted it for him and Melissa.

At every turn, he seemed to sabotage any chance of convincing Mel to marry him. Watching Melissa's face crumple when Mr. Shimizu revealed his plan to move to Austin made it clear he should have discussed the move with her first.

He'd kept the job change secret, not to blindside her, but to avoid disappointing her if the transfer didn't work out. And it turned out he didn't have to worry about it anyway. Both of them were disappointed now.

He wished he could explain. But did he have a good reason to hold back the information? The answer was no. She was more discreet than anyone else he knew.

Now his biggest fear was that she was in the process of packing her bags, finding a ride back to Petaluma, and taking to the air before he could justify his rationale for not telling her.

His shoulder and back muscles ached. Theresa curved her hand under his elbow, nudging him along until they got to the resort restaurant's bar.

"Two whiskeys, neat." She didn't bother getting his approval for the drink order, handing him one of the glasses and then leading the way to a sitting area in an alcove off of the main lobby area. At any other time, he'd say the fireplace-lit nook was intimate and cozy, but not tonight. Tonight, he felt chilled to his marrow.

"Sit down." Theresa clearly had her mother hat on because her tone reminded him of his mom chiding him when he hadn't done his assigned chores.

"I appreciate—"

"Brian, please sit. Just give me five minutes. Please."

He lowered himself into one of the overstuffed round leather chairs and stared into the gas fireplace flames that also illuminated the compassionate gleam in Theresa's eyes.

"I don't usually butt into other people's business, but you and Melissa seem to be having some trouble."

"You could say that." Brian took a long swallow of whiskey and allowed the burn to be his well-deserved punishment for the stress and anxiety he was causing Melissa.

"She's not like the other women you've dated, and based on the engagement ring she's wearing, your intentions toward her are different as well." Theresa rubbed her bare arms, the glass of whiskey sitting untouched on the side table.

"Do you want me to go get your wrap?" He started to stand, but she put a hand on his shoulder and pushed him back into the chair.

"I can endure five minutes of shivering in support of true love."

"True love?" Brian resolved to listen carefully to what his friend had to say. "I'm not so sure."

"I'm sure. The way she looks at you says it all, but you must stop treating Melissa like a china doll. You can't make decisions for her or make decisions without her input. You also can't put her on a shelf so she's safe and protected until you want to play with her."

"You don't—"

"Just listen." She leaned forward and placed a hand on his forearm. "You don't have to agree or disagree. I'd like to offer you a different perspective that may help you both."

He leaned against the leather and made a "go on" motion with the glass of whiskey.

"Melissa is a strong, independent woman. She's built a life and a career for herself, by herself. Now you're calling the shots, making the decisions, thinking for her. Marty told me you've been best friends for years, which is a fabulous foundation for marriage, but you've gone from friend to fiancé overnight. That kind of adjustment takes time."

Brian let Theresa's words sink in. "So, you think I'm rushing it?"

"Melissa is a warrior—bold, brave, fierce. And after talking to her over lunch, I've come to the conclusion she'll fight for what matters and for what she wants. But she's also a woman—passionate and, believe it or not, vulnerable and tender. You need to find a balance between the two halves of her whole. Show her you cherish her just as much as you respect her. Relationships are rarely fifty-fifty, but both partners should have an equal say in things."

"I only wanted to help, to make things easier for her." Brian tossed back the rest of the whiskey.

"Tell her that. Then solve the rest of the problems together."

Brian leaned forward, but Theresa blocked him again, chuckling softly. "I'm not done."

"You said five minutes," Brian grumbled, but there was no selfish complaint in his voice.

"Melissa is struggling with her own issues. She mentioned earlier that she's never been married, never had a long-term romantic relationship, and never dated seriously. She doesn't know how to let a man into her life. She doesn't know how to be soft, feminine, flirtatious, and, I expect, sexy. I assume she's familiar with some of the women you've dated in the past?"

He nodded.

"You brought some of them to company picnics and cookouts at our place, so I know your type, too. Young, sexy, out for a good time. Perhaps Melissa thinks that's the type of woman she has to become to make you happy."

"That's ridiculous. If I wanted a woman like that, would I have asked Melissa to marry me?"

"There's a compliment in there somewhere...I think." Theresa cocked her head. "Let's recap."

"Melissa is strong and independent. Decisions should be made with her, not for her."

"Great. What else?"

"Melissa is soft and strong, independent and vulnerable, a warrior and a woman. I need to honor all parts of her."

"Keep going."

"Melissa's never dated or had a boyfriend. I need to court her. Woo her. Make her fall in love with me."

"Oh, dear. You were doing so well. I thought you were going to ace the final exam." Humor glinted in Theresa's expression.

"Which part did I get wrong?" Frustration nibbled at the edges of the confidence that had been building as a result of Theresa's wise advice.

"I've seen the way Melissa looks at you." Theresa raised her crystal lowball glass in a congratulatory salute. "She's already in love. Melissa fell in love with you a long time ago."

The villa was dark when Brian let himself in an hour later. Melissa hadn't even left a table lamp on, but relief flooded him when he spotted her shoes on the floor by the couch. She hadn't packed and left.

He debated whether he should confront her now or wait until morning, then went with his gut.

He knocked firmly on her bedroom door. "Melissa. We need to talk."

He waited as long as his patience would allow, then he knocked again.

"Melissa, please. I don't want to go to bed until we resolve this."

The bedclothes rustled, but still she didn't open the door.

He knocked again—politely and steadily—until the heavy door yanked open just enough for her to peek out at him.

"Stop with the knocking." Her eyes and nose were red from crying.

He felt like getting on the floor and crawling around like the slug that he was in hopes that she might laugh.

He'd royally screwed up this time.

"I don't want to talk to you right now. You made me cry,

and I don't cry. Ever. I'm angry and might say something I'll regret." She sniffled.

"We've always been able to say anything to each other."

"That was when we were *friends*."

"We're not friends anymore?" He kept his voice low, hoping it would draw her out.

"I don't know what we are." She threw the door wide and stalked into the small living area, keeping the coffee table between them.

God, she was beautiful, with her hazel eyes glimmering with emotion, high cheekbones, and toned limbs. Her misery only made her more precious to him. He wanted to soothe away her angst, put her mind at ease, reassure her everything would work out.

"We'll always be friends, Mel. No matter what else happens." Brian rubbed at the oncoming headache with the heel of one hand. "I apologize, *again*, for not telling you about the job in Austin. I didn't want to say anything until I knew it was an option. I wasn't trying to go behind your back, and as it turns out, the job is already taken."

"It wouldn't have resolved anything even if you did get the job." Melissa's shoulders sagged, and her voice lost its strident edge. "After I got a clear medical report, I told my commanding officer that I wanted to get transferred back to a fighter wing. He's looking into it, but I could be in San Antonio for another year…or another month. I just don't know."

"Okay. So you get transferred. We'll work it out, Mel. We've always been good at working things out."

"What? Are you going to keep changing jobs to follow me around the country, maybe around the world? There has to be a compromise, and my question is which one of us is going to have to make the compromise?"

"I get it. Theresa gave me a little talking-to. Making

decisions without your input was a mistake." Emotion constricted his throat. "I was trying to make everything easier for you, and all I did was earn your distrust. You've been through so much with the cancer diagnosis and your DNIF status. You must be incredibly frustrated."

She bristled, her spine straightening, inadvertently thrusting her chest out, eyes narrowing into slits, jaw clenching. "I'm coping just fine."

Something clicked in Brian's head. "Are you fine? Really, Mel? You don't think I'm judging you or criticizing you for how you're handling things?"

"That's what it sounds like."

"Well, I'm not. But how do you think I feel? Every time I've offered to fly down, take you to your treatments, or stay with you afterward, you rejected my offer. I can't love you if you don't let me in, Mel."

He crossed the room in three steps and banded his hands around her upper arms, forcing her to meet his eyes. "You think I'm judging you when I'm trying to protect you and take care of you."

"I can take care of myself." She jerked out of his grasp. "I've been taking care of myself since the day my father died. And the military has certainly proved I'm capable."

Click. Ah, so that was the problem.

Her dad had been her whole life. She cherished him. When he died, she blamed him for leaving. And blamed her mom next, for getting married again. He was certain she'd lost a few close friends in the military as well.

The logical side of Melissa knew her father's death was accidental, but the little girl who still lived inside believed her father deserted her. Then there were her friends who hadn't made it back home. That had to have taken a toll.

"BestE, I, of all people, know how capable you are. You can, and do, take care of yourself. But I want to help. It's that guy gene that makes me want to be your hero. It's an honor and privilege to be entrusted with the well-being of someone you care about.

"When you refused to let me come help while you were undergoing treatment, it hurt. A lot. All I could do was sit by the phone and wait, and I have to tell you, it sucked."

Tears glimmered along the edge of her lashes, and pain darkened her eyes.

"I don't know how to let you love me." Her anguished admission, so low he barely heard it, made his eyes sting.

"I've royally pissed you off twice in a single day, so I'd say I have plenty to learn myself." Brian folded her against him and held on with everything he had. "We can figure this out, Mel. I know we can. It's love, not rocket science."

Chapter 7

"Mel, please wear the ring."

Brian pushed the red velvet box back across the bistro table in their villa. Not wanting to go out, he'd ordered two continental breakfasts and a large carafe of coffee. It was going to be a long day of meetings, and he wanted to make sure she was okay, meaning she wasn't having any more regrets, before he left for his scheduled, day-long retreat activities.

She slid the small box back to the edge of the tan placemat. "Not until it's official."

"We talked about this last night."

The box went back to her side of the table, but she immediately nudged it back.

"What we *agreed*"—she emphasized—"was to take as much time as either of us needs to feel comfortable as boyfriend and girlfriend before committing to marriage."

"You know we're going to end up together." He toyed with his fork. "I don't want to wait. Besides, we're too old to be boyfriend and girlfriend."

"Says you." She gave him one of her "general glares" that

would have made most people shudder, but he knew her. "I've never had a boyfriend, a true boyfriend. I want to simply enjoy this courtship for a while. Besides, your original proposal wasn't very romantic. 'Wear this beautiful ring while we decide if we want our temporary engagement to be permanent.' I don't want to feel like your fake fiancée."

"That's the best excuse you've come up with so far. I can't argue with you on that point." Brian covered her hand with his. "I'll keep this…for now. But someday it's going back on your finger."

"Come up with something more creative than the parking lot of a regional airport and maybe I'll say yes."

He sighed and rubbed his sleep-deprived eyes. They'd been up until three a.m. First talking, then cuddling in front of the fireplace, then making out like horny teenagers.

In the span of four hours, he'd gone through bone-jarring emotions that launched him into the stars and then into the depths of a dark, bottomless pit. The past hour had been spent trying to find the right words to express his thoughts and feelings, while struggling to understand where Melissa was coming from.

"Oh, man." He set his phone back on the table. "I need to leave or Erickson will ride me the rest of the weekend." He stood and set his dishes in the sink. "What are your plans for the day?"

Her eyes shifted guiltily. "Not much. Maybe a mani/pedi with Theresa. That sounds fun."

She was such a bad liar.

"There's also a nature hike," she added.

That was more like it.

But he decided not to call her out on a little white lie. It wasn't worth it. He'd find out soon enough how she spent her day. They both knew how dangerous secrets were, but a surprise now and then kept life interesting.

"We'll be done by five. Most of the attendees are attending a wine-tasting at the resort's vineyard, so I thought it'd be a great time for us to spend the evening together. Just the two of us." He leaned down to retrieve his computer tablet and bag.

"I'd like that." Melissa rose and walked with him to the front door of the villa.

"I wish I could stay," he said, knowing he was already late. Erickson was going to have something to say. He always did. But Melissa was here right now, soft and warm. He placed a gentle kiss on her lips. "Have fun, dear."

She giggled, and the sound was magical. Some things in life were priceless.

Pleasing Erickson wasn't one of them.

As soon as Brian was gone, Melissa finished dressing and hurried up to the resort's main building to see if she could find the concierge. She had a birthday celebration to organize and hoped some of the resort staff would help out.

At the front desk, she explained her dilemma. The sweet-faced young woman, about twenty-five years old, suggested she meet with Zoey Foster, the Silver Fox Resort owner, since Amy Denham, the resort's event coordinator, was off-site.

Probably at the big meeting Brian went to.

After a short wait, Melissa was led back to the owner's office. Besides being comfortably appointed and well-organized, the room featured a stunning panorama of the ocean and coastline.

"I could stand here and admire the view all day." Zoey, who was a little younger than Melissa, turned from the window and sat into the chair behind her desk. She grabbed a pen and tapped it against the wooden surface, revealing carefully restrained nerves. "You're in one of the Sea View villas, right? How do you like it?"

"Like you just said, I could enjoy the view all day." Melissa moved to the edge of her seat. "You're incredibly lucky to call this place home."

"I grew up here with my sister and brothers and never wanted to live anywhere else. Where are you from?"

"I'm not really *from* anywhere. I'm a Navy brat. My father was stationed at bases around the world."

"You traded Navy for Air Force, right?" When Melissa smiled blankly, Zoey chuckled. "Silver Fox is a small resort, and we pride ourselves on knowing our guests and providing them with an environment where they can relax. And, from time to time, word gets around. Not in a bad way. A more discreet, whispered way. I heard about the stunning, newly engaged, female fighter pilot staying with us from the restaurant waitstaff. There was some kind of announcement in the dining room yesterday?"

"That announcement was premature and not approved for release." Melissa grimaced ruefully. "I'm here with a long-time friend. We think our relationship has the potential for more, and this weekend is sort of a trial run."

"That's an unusual approach to determining compatibility, but if it works..." Zoey shrugged. "Now. Stacy says you needed some help with something. A birthday party? The dining room might be booked, but I'll check."

"I had something different in mind. My...friend and I share the same birthday. We turn fifty tomorrow, but I wanted to surprise him with a special dinner tonight. Something private, at our villa."

Zoey stopped tapping and poised the pen over a notepad bearing the resort logo. "Not a problem. I'll have our Events

Coordinator come up with some decorations, and Nate…the chef…will create a one-of-a-kind menu. He's good at that sort of thing. Let me take some notes while we're talking."

Something warm and fuzzy unfurled in Melissa's chest. She'd never planned a surprise party or organized a special event for someone. No baby showers or bachelorette parties. No Thanksgiving dinners or Christmas brunches. She didn't even put thought into gifts for her mother, simply requesting an attractive floral arrangement for birthdays, Mother's Days, and holidays.

Like a thump between the eyes, everything Brian tried to tell her last night became crystal clear.

It's a privilege to be entrusted with the well-being of someone you care about.

Regret seeped in. She'd wanted to show everyone how strong she was. That was the military way. However, by refusing Brian's offer of help during her cancer treatments, she not only withheld the privilege of trusting him but also rejected his expression of caring and concern. She'd rejected his love.

She'd been rejecting her mother's love and concern as well.

Melissa prided herself on her strength and independence, but in truth, she was scared. She was protecting herself from being hurt or disappointed. If she kept people out, they couldn't hurt her, or she them. She risked her life every time she got in a jet, yet she didn't have the courage to risk her feelings or her heart.

Not even with the people closest to her.

"Miss Davenport? Melissa?"

Zoey was waiting for an answer of some sort. Stunned by her realizations, she filed the points away for further examination.

"I'm sorry. What did you ask?"

"Is the menu I've put together acceptable? The three-course meal will include a bottle of wine from my brother's vineyard and a birthday cake for two."

She scanned the handwritten menu and nodded. *Brian will love it.*

"I'll let Amy know as soon as she's back, and we'll get started on those decorations. I'm thinking fresh flowers, candles, and maybe a few strands of lights." Zoey pushed back from her desk.

Melissa pictured Brian's reaction and smiled. "Thank you so much for handling this."

"Oh, I'm happy to help. We love taking care of our guests, and it's so much easier when we know exactly what they want." Zoey winked and followed her toward the door. "If I don't see you, have a happy birthday."

Anticipation surged through Melissa.

She just hoped Brian didn't mind her surprise.

Chapter 8

The minute hand passed five o'clock, then five fifteen, five thirty.

Damn Erickson. You said that three times already. Give us a break.

At five forty, Erickson was still rambling about restructuring the company according to specialties versus projects when Mr. Shimizu finally cut him off—in a very proper and respectful manner, of course. As soon as the meeting ended, Brian was up and out of his seat with computer tablet and bag in hand.

"A moment, Mr. Newbury," Mr. Shimizu called and followed him out of the conference room. "May I have an additional moment of your time?"

Mr. Shimizu walked down the travertine-tiled hall, peeked into an empty meeting room, and beckoned Brian inside. Brian's heart was going a mile a minute, and he hoped Erikson hadn't thrown him under the bus again. Erickson had a habit of driving over the top of his employees every chance he got and then backing over them just to make sure they were locked in place.

"I'd like to continue our discussion from last night." Mr. Shimizu bowed slightly.

Brian returned the gesture, but his bow was more stiff than fluid.

"I feel it important to relay that, while we have already hired someone for the Global Environmental Program position, Daebak has something in the works for which I believe you are uniquely qualified."

Brian stared at the door, distracted. Melissa was waiting for him. Then he mentally shook himself and returned his attention to Mr. Shimizu. "Interesting. I'd like to hear more."

"I sense some urgency in your desire to leave, so I will keep this short. Daebak wants to launch a new division that would make us competitive in the aerospace industry. Think private satellites, space transportation services, exploration, and colonization. You began your career at NASA. We need someone like you to guide the development of DaeSky."

"What? Wow!" His brain froze, then kicked into overdrive, considering the implications of Mr. Shimizu's revelation. "That sounds exciting." Space exploration was exactly why he went into engineering in the first place. He wanted to put a man on Mars. "I'd love to hear more." Now the man had his full attention.

"May I send over an information packet?"

"Absolutely."

"You are an asset to our company, Mr. Newbury, and we want to make sure you are happy."

Brian gazed at Mr. Shimizu, processing what the Japanese CEO just said. This was the chance of a lifetime he'd been waiting for, and he hoped Melissa agreed. "Thank you, sir. That is good to hear."

"Very good. I'll have a prospectus delivered before nine p.m., and I will make myself available tomorrow in case you have questions. I know how frustrating it can be to wait for answers."

"I'm honored you thought of me, Mr. Shimizu, and I understand the confidentiality required for something like this. Would it be acceptable to share the basics with Ms. Davenport? She has top-level military clearance, but more importantly, I've promised her all decisions concerning our future will be made together."

"Of course. My wife would expect the same. Just so you know, the location for the DaeSky facility has not yet been selected. We are looking at sites in Florida and Texas. The development committee will come back with their recommendations next month," Mr. Shimizu bowed his head and then held out his hand. "Have a pleasant evening, and please give my best to Miss Davenport."

Brian shook the executive's hand and then practically ran out of the retreat lodge into the dark autumn evening. He couldn't wait to share the news with Melissa.

The garden path to the villas was busy with foot traffic. He passed several couples strolling along on their way to dinner or the evening's wine tasting. It was several minutes before he charged through the door and skidded to a halt.

A large banner announcing HAPPY BIRTHDAY! hung over the fireplace. Short and tall candles arranged throughout the living room filled the space with flickering light that danced on the walls. The table was set with crystal and china, the tantalizing aromas of herbs and spices scenting the air.

Melissa stepped out of her bedroom with a tremulous smile.

"Surprise!"

"Oh, babe. This is…this is amazing. How did you—"

"While you were retreating, I was organizing."

He took a deep breath to calm his racing heart and focus his attention where it belonged—on Melissa.

Crossing the room, he reached for her hand. "Let me look at you."

She twirled slowly, dipping under his arm, giving him a leisurely view of her dress.

He'd never seen her in something so scrumptiously sexy. The metallic silver dress hugged every inch of her, accentuating her curves, ending mid-thigh to reveal mile-long legs. The short, fashionable haircut showed off her long neck and the sparkling crystal earrings that almost touched her shoulders—very unusual for her.

"New earrings?"

She blushed. "You noticed. I don't get to wear fancy jewelry. It's against code." She shrugged. "I saw this pair in the gift shop and thought I would splurge. Do you really like them?"

"They are beautiful, but you, my love, are a knockout."

Her blush deepened. She gestured toward the table. "The resort chef prepared a special meal, just for us. Why don't I open a bottle of wine while you take a few minutes to relax? The food's in the warmer." She pointed to a trolley with a stainless-steel metal box on the bottom. He wondered what was under the other two metal covered domes sitting in the tray on top but was willing to wait for her to reveal the surprise. "We can eat at any time."

"You are wonderful." Brian kissed her cheek and headed into his room.

Fifteen minutes later he had showered, shaved, brushed his teeth, and changed into a white Oxford shirt and black trousers. He slapped on cologne, swiped a comb through his hair, and sprinted back to the living room to find Melissa lounging on the couch with a short pour of wine in her hand.

She looked up, her eyes brightening, her smile widening at the sight of him. "You look nice."

She set her glass of wine down, kicked off her silver heels, and padded over in bare feet. Even without the added height of the shoes, she came up to his chin. And when she wrapped her arms around his waist and burrowed close, she was a perfect fit.

"You smell nice," she murmured, pressing kisses along his jaw. "You feel nice. You taste nice. You are nice. So nice."

"Wow." This sexy seductress was the second surprise of the day, and Brian felt a little off-kilter. "This is not how I expected to celebrate our fiftieth."

"It's not officially our birthday. That's tomorrow. You have retreat obligations, and I have to fly back, so I thought we should celebrate early to make the most of this very special occasion."

"It's not every day you turn fifty with your best friend."

"I thought I was your girlfriend." She chucked him under the chin playfully.

"You're my everything." Brian grew serious. "My study buddy. My best friend. My girlfriend. And, I hope one day, my wife."

"I'm getting used to the idea." She moved away to retrieve their wine glasses.

Brian sat at one end of the couch and patted the space next to him. She passed him one of the glasses and then snuggled under his arm, her back to his front.

"More importantly, I think I'm figuring out how this stuff works." She took a sip as if gathering her thoughts. "When I was planning this surprise, I kept thinking about your reaction and how pleased you'd be. I wanted you to know how special you are to me. Going to the effort of organizing a birthday dinner was my way of showing you how much you matter. I had an epiphany while you were gone. I believe

I now understand why you needed to help when I was dealing with my cancer diagnosis and treatment."

"When I found out about your cancer, I panicked. Suddenly, I realized you might not always be there for me. I think that's when I first got the idea of proposing marriage." He smoothed back her short hair, feeling the new, soft strands of re-growth. "I hate that you went through the chemo and radiation treatments alone. What if the outcome had been less positive? What if the cancer had been terminal? I couldn't stand the thought of you dying alone. The thought of losing you is unbearable. My life wouldn't be the same without you."

When she didn't respond, Brian tried to lighten the mood. "But today is a new start—for both of us. I'm willing to wait until you've had enough girlfriend and boyfriend time and you're ready to spend the rest of our lives together."

"I never imagined our friendship turning into marriage." She sighed. "Funny how everything has circled back to graduation night and that silly promise we made." She looked at him. "In retrospect, maybe it wasn't so silly after all."

"Yes, but you barely tolerated me until you discovered we were both born on December first. Then it was game on." His gaze once again swept over the flower arrangements, candles, and huge sign. "This is the perfect way to kick off the holiday season."

He shifted the angle of their hug so he could meet her eyes. "Hey, I have an idea. Why don't you fly up to Denver and celebrate Christmas with me at my parents' place? I already promised to spend the week between Christmas and New Year's with them. They'd love to see you and ask about you all the time. And...maybe we'll have some news to share with them by then."

Warm feelings rose and relaxed him while he imagined his family's reaction when he and Melissa announced their official engagement. Even if she refused to wear his ring, it was just a matter of time…

"Are you ready to eat? Chef Nate prepared a feast. Chateaubriand with Bearnaise sauce, scalloped potatoes, lemony broccolini, and a double-chocolate torte. The kitchen even included a birthday candle. A big, red 5-0."

"My mouth is watering. Here, let me pour the wine."

"Why, thank you, sir."

"The resort manager thought of everything. She even sent up extra bottles of wine and water, and Amy, the Events Coordinator, pulled all this together in just a couple of hours. I think she outdid herself with the decorations."

"You're the one who made this happen. This night is perfect. Thank you." He held up his glass to her. "To us."

"To us." She set her wine glass down and bent to pull the plates out of the warmer using the fancy resort heat glove.

"Oh, doesn't this smell good?" She set the plate cover aside.

He reached for her hand and brought her wrist to his nose. "Yes. You smell good enough to eat."

She planted a kiss on his forehead. "Later." Her eyes held a promise. "I'm starved."

The savory dinner didn't have a chance. The plates were quickly emptied. "That was amazing, but now I'm stuffed." He went to the built-in sound system and turned up the music, a mix of slow jams and ballads, that had played during dinner. "May I have this dance?

Her eyes glittered, but she stepped into his arms with another tremulous smile.

He lost track of time as they swayed together. He stroked the satiny skin exposed by her dress…her shoulders, the bumps along her spine, her arms, her neck. He memorized the flowery scent of her perfume, the barely audible sigh that escaped her when he caressed a sensitive patch of skin, and the reassuring press of her body against his.

She was still here.

They still had time.

Together.

A quick knock sounded from the front door, interrupting the blissful interlude. He looked at her in puzzlement.

"Did you call the kitchen?"

"Not yet."

"Ah, I know who it is. Mr. Shimizu promised to drop off some paperwork."

Eager for Melissa to return to his embrace, Brian rushed to the door while he pulled a five-dollar bill from his money clip. He opened the door to hand the bellman the money in exchange for a large manila envelope.

"It must be important." Melissa stood behind the couch, a pensive expression darkening her face.

"Mr. Shimizu pulled me aside today. Daebak is getting ready to enter the private aerospace industry. He wants me to join the executive leadership team, said my experience at NASA would be critical to the success of the company's new venture."

"It sounds like the job was custom-made for you." Her tone was light and airy, but her arms were now crossed, and he felt her backing away even though her feet weren't moving.

She was shutting down. Closing him out. Again.

"Mel." He placed the packet on the hall table. "I haven't accepted the job. He hasn't even made a formal offer. He wanted to give me a heads-up so when the time comes, you and I can make a decision together."

"There's no decision to be made." Melissa's unhappiness was vivid in the downward curve of her mouth and the frown lines across her forehead. "It's a no-brainer. You'd be crazy to turn down an opportunity like this. That job puts a pretty little bow on everything you've dreamed of and what you've already achieved. It will mark the pinnacle of your career."

"Why do I get the impression you believe I have to choose between this job or you?"

"Take the job." She took a step back when he approached. "It's perfect for you. And let's be honest. You'll be a hundred percent focused on starting up the company. I've been on projects like this. They are all-consuming."

"Your job is just as demanding. If a conflict breaks out somewhere in the world, you'd be off like a rocket. Why do we have to choose between our jobs and each other? We can have both. Other people make it work. Why can't we?" He mirrored her defensive posture, folding his arms and bracing his feet.

"Because two people dedicating all their energies toward their jobs is not how relationships work, Brian. Relationships take time and effort, none of which either of us will have."

"Would it be so bad if you quit your job?" He raked his fingers through his hair. "I know you're bored. Why don't you get a government consulting job? You could work from anywhere."

"I didn't work my butt off to become one of the top fighter pilots in the Air Force to just give it all up on a whim!"

He reared back as if she'd slapped him. "This relationship is not a whim. It's been on a long simmer, and it's time to turn up the heat. We deserve to be together." He reached for her hand. "Besides, you wouldn't be giving up anything. There are plenty of well-paid government contractors. Heck, you could go work for the company working on the Next Generation Air Dominance program. I'm sure they'd love to have you on board." He squeezed her fingers. "Either way, we can still be married, and you would be *my* wife."

Melissa shook her head. "This isn't going to work."

"Why, Mel? Why isn't it going to work?"

"Because you are asking me to bend too far. I'm not willing to give up everything I've worked so hard to achieve."

"I'm not asking you to give anything up."

"You just asked me to consider taking a consulting job, leave my military family." Her laser-sharp glare stung. "It's clear you want this job, so take it. You've worked hard and deserve it."

"Mel…" His body tensed with an urgent plea.

"Brian, don't second guess this." She backed away. "Take the job. It's the right thing to do." Her eyes met his.

"I want you to be my wife. If I can't have that, then I'll take whatever you have to give."

"Right now, I need space. I'll get a room up at the resort building. Please call the Front Desk and have my things sent over."

"What about us?" He moved in closer.

His heart ached when she took another step back. "Don't push, Brian. I don't want to lose our friendship, but I need some time to sort out my feelings."

He could see on her face that he'd already lost. He could do nothing to keep her, so he did the only thing left to do. He stepped back and put his hands in his pockets. "I will wait for you, Mel. I'll wait forever if that's what it takes."

A lifeless smile crossed her face. "You might think that today, but soon you'll start on a new project and get lost in all the details. The days will pass, and time will become a blur in the excitement of building something new. You'll forget to call your parents. You'll miss birthdays. Your friends will wonder why you haven't called in months."

That might be true, but she would always be his number one priority.

He wanted to express his love for her, but she wouldn't hear it. She'd already put on her bulletproof vest where any kindness would ricochet away.

Which left him with only one option. "Okay, Mel. We'll do this your way."

"Take care, Brian." She kissed him on the cheek.

His heart broke open, and the pain shot across his chest. He could do nothing but watch while she walked out of his life.

Chapter 9

Three Weeks Later

Refilling her wine glass, Melissa stared at the three-foot artificial tree she'd set up in her front window and debated the merits of white lights or multicolored lights. She bought both, along with tinsel, candy canes, and silver and gold glass bulbs.

"Alexa, play Brian's Favorite Holiday Tunes."

She hadn't planned to decorate, but the only thing worse than being alone during the holidays was being alone and lonely.

Since walking out on Brian three weeks ago, she'd been miserable. Her military training made it easy to mask her feelings. Way too easy. No one at work was surprised when she only put in an appearance at the professionally required parties. The only person who knew her well enough to notice something was wrong was Brian, and they weren't talking.

Her choice, not his.

He called.

He texted.

He emailed.

He'd even mailed her a handwritten letter with a stamp in the upper right corner and return address in the left. It sat, unopened, propped against the tiny wooden jewelry box where she kept the diamond earrings from her father.

She had to give Brian points for persistence. He kept trying her at different times throughout the day, emailing short messages like "I just need to know you're okay," and "I miss you. Want to talk?" and "If friendship is all you can give me, I'll take it."

To answer his question, she wasn't okay. She missed him so much it hurt. She wanted to give him what he needed but deep down she couldn't.

Mr. Shimizu's offer was a once-in-a-lifetime opportunity for Brian. It was like a world-class athlete who'd trained for the Olympics and then walked away from the starting line. She couldn't ask him to sacrifice a position like this or stand in his way. He had to take the job.

She loved him too much to stand in his way.

God, she missed her bestie. He was the guy who helped her through times like this. He was her rock. Her touchstone. Her voice of reason. Too bad this time he was probably the only one who could help her heal her broken heart.

Ignoring her buzzing phone, at least *pretending* to ignore the incoming call, she chose a strand of multicolored lights and began winding them around the tree limbs. When the three strands were hung, she plugged them in. The twinkling bursts of color lifted her mood a fraction of an inch.

Her phone chimed again, announcing the caller had left a voice mail. She opened the package of red-and-white striped candy canes and carefully hung them amid the lights.

When the phone rang again, she dropped the box of tinsel, silver strands slithering across the floor.

Hands trembling, she checked the phone. Worry followed on the heels of relief. It was her mother. They weren't due for another call until Christmas, three days away.

"Hi, Mom. Is everything okay?"

"Mel, honey." Her mom was crying, sniffling, trying to get the words out.

"Mom, what happened? What's wrong?" She forgot the silly tree and Brian to focus on her mother's voice and lowered onto the couch cushions.

"Honey, I…got your…Christmas gift today."

"Is that why you're crying?" Melissa released a breath of relief. "I didn't expect this reaction."

"I haven't been able to get past the first few pages. The memory book is so…" her mother sobbed again, "…it's truly special. It seems I've missed a lot."

Melissa thought of the hours it took to select just the right pictures that would tell a story and to arrange them in a meaningful way. She wanted her mom to know who she was, not the child she'd abandoned, but the military professional, the one who still needed her mom.

"Oh, Mom. Don't cry."

"I missed your graduation from college and flight school. I missed your promotion ceremonies. And to see those pictures of you in Afghanistan—well, I'm just going to say I'm glad you're home safe."

Life didn't offer do-overs, but it offered second chances, and Melissa was making the most of a second chance to build a relationship with her mom.

"I don't know how to thank you, dear."

"You just did."

Melissa hadn't forgotten the lessons learned with Brian at Silver Fox Resort. Over the years, she'd robbed her mother of so many possible moments and memories because of the wound created when her father died.

That was going to change.

She had already planned a visit for February.

"Your dad would be so proud of you." Another sniffle. "I'm proud of you, too. You've accomplished so much."

"Not as much as I would have liked."

"Aw, honey. Regrets are so hard to live with, but we all have our share. I wish your father hadn't died so young. I regret not being a better mom when you needed me. I miss being close and sharing the little, everyday moments with you.

"Some regrets are unavoidable, but some are ones we create. There's nothing anyone could have done to save your father, but I could have reached out to you instead of waiting for you to come to me. I kept hoping one day you'd be ready. Then, before I knew it, the gap between us was so wide I didn't know how to close the distance. I decided maybe you were better off without me complicating your life."

"Mom, you're not a complication." Now they were both sniffling. "Life is never easy. It's always complicated."

"Then you forgive me?"

"There's nothing to forgive." She let a little pride slip in. "Besides, I didn't turn out so bad."

"No." Her mom blew her nose. "No, you didn't. In fact, you've made something spectacular out of your life. And thank you, honey, for the memory book. I love you."

"I love you, too, Mom. Talk to you on Christmas."

"I can't wait. Bye, honey."

Melissa ended the call and wiped away a tear.

What was up with all the tears lately? She never cried. Then again, maybe she should once in a while.

She breathed out a sigh. For so many years she'd

crammed her memories in a mental box and kept them hidden.

Her dad's death. Her mom's remarriage. The horrors she'd seen in the battle zone. Her cancer scare. The list went on and on. The list of buried feelings was immense.

At least she'd finally made progress with her mom. And to think her mom hadn't reached out to her because she believed Melissa would be better off without having her mom intrude in her life. But that was the furthest thing from the truth.

The false belief had cost them both.

She made a commitment, right then, to open up to her mom more, even if exposing herself was going to be hard. Being vulnerable was the cost of living and loving.

Her heart twisted as her mind expanded to encompass a new version of reality.

Like mother, like daughter.

She was repeating her mother's mistake.

She made the same decision for Brian, believing she was sparing him the pain of deciding between her and his career.

The engagement was off, but hopefully there was time to save their friendship. Without Brian, there were no complications. No life. No love.

It was time for an honest, in-depth conversation.

hristmas Eve

Brian flipped through channels, not really seeing the images on his sixty-inch screen. Soccer games. Home shopping channels. Celebrities making cookies. Santa Claus, elves, and parades.

He could have been celebrating with his parents and brother in Denver instead of sitting in the dark by himself, but that would have required pretending.

He'd tried that.

For the past twenty-three days, he pretended Mel hadn't rejected him. He pretended it didn't matter they hadn't spoken. He pretended his heart wasn't broken. He pretended he could live without his BestE. But he was still just pretending.

When his phone rang, he snatched it up, hoping it was Mel only to discover it was Marty. Disappointment landed with a thud on his chest.

"Hey, Brian. Merry Christmas, buddy."

"Merry Christmas to you, too."

"You're still moping, aren't you?" Marty's sigh was audible. "Why don't you come over and celebrate with us? There's plenty of food."

"No, man. I'm good. You enjoy your time with your family."

There was a hesitation on the phone. "Did you decide whether or not you were going to accept the job?"

"Not yet." He huffed out a breath. "I'm not sure I want to help stand up another company. Erickson sure hasn't appreciated all my hard work. Besides, what are we working so hard for? Our state-of-the-art equipment is just going to be obsolete in twelve months, maybe less. And every day there's new young talent ascending through the ranks, convinced our ideas are old and outdated. I don't know, man. Some days, I feel ancient."

"That's 'cause you are." Marty snorted a laugh.

"Jerk." Brian managed a chuckle. "I don't want to grow old alone or settle for someone who's almost Melissa. I want her in my life, in any capacity, and I can't figure out how the hell to make that happen."

"I won't even ask how many times you've called her. I'm sure it's well over a dozen."

"Try twelve dozen."

Marty laughed. "Come over, buddy. There's a beer with your name on it."

"I'm okay. I've got a movie ready to stream." At least that was true. *It's A Wonderful Life* was one of Melissa's favorites, although he hadn't yet come up with enough courage to watch it. "Maybe we can do something for New Year's."

"Okay." Marty didn't hide his disappointment. "Oh, and Brian?"

"Yeah, man?"

"I concur. A job is never worth it in the long run. You accept a job thinking it's going to be your crowning achievement, and after a few months, the job starts to feel like all the other jobs. There are politics, deadlines, and budget issues everywhere. It all becomes a blur until you walk in your front door and you hear scampering feet and see the woman you love with a smile on her face. That's what makes life worthwhile."

His heart squeezed at the simple truth of what Marty said. "I hear you, man. I need to give you credit. You're pretty smart for figuring all that out on your own." Brian chuckled.

"I always knew I was smarter than you. Better looking, too."

"But you still love me." The remark sounded flippant, but he knew it to be true. Marty had his back. Always had. Just like Melissa. "I'll catch ya later. Give my love to your family."

The phone call disconnected.

God, he missed her.

The day before his birthday—*their* birthday—sitting in the Daebak retreat, he daydreamed about skiing at Steamboat Springs with Melissa, convincing his mother to teach her how to make *Apfelkuchen*, curling up in front of the fireplace after everyone else went to bed, and welcoming the New Year with a kiss under the mistletoe.

Those daydreams followed him home and turned to nightmares, taunting him while he slept.

As tortured as he was by his own loss, what pained him the most were thoughts of Melissa continuing to go through life alone. She deserved so much more. If not from him, then a man who would love her and adore her at least half as much as he did.

He pressed the remote, frowning when the doorbell chimed. He considered ignoring it, suspecting it was Bob, his next-door neighbor, wanting permission for holiday party guests to park in his driveway. When the bell sounded a second, then third time, he sighed and rolled off the couch.

He apparently wasn't moving fast enough because Bob started knocking.

"Hold on, I'm com—" Tugging the door open, he discovered it wasn't Bob. "Melissa." He looked behind her at the taxi driving away.

Every cell, every organ in his body stalled, unable to move or speak.

"May I come in?" Dressed in an ivy green sweater, scarf printed with holly berries, blue jeans, and black ankle boots, she carried a small overnighter. She looked good…except for the dark circles under her eyes and sunken cheeks.

Still speechless, he opened the door and stood back.

"I thought you were spending Christmas with your family in Denver," she said.

"Change of plans." His voice cracked like it wasn't getting much use, probably because he didn't feel like talking to anyone. Anyone except Melissa.

"Your parents send their love." She set her bag down beside the couch and looked around, taking in the beige walls, tan carpet, and brown furniture.

Wait a minute… His parents sent their love?

"When did you see my parents?" He closed the door and flipped the lock, following her into the living room.

"This morning."

"You were in Denver this morning?"

"Yes, Brian. I flew up to surprise you. I would have been here earlier, but I had to refuel and file another flight plan. It's a good thing the weather cooperated, or I would have ended up spending Christmas with your folks. I like them, but I love you more. By the way, I didn't think a home could lack more personality than mine, but your place is a beige shoebox."

He shoved his hands in his pockets and looked around. The description fit. "I don't spend a lot of time here."

Wait. Press rewind. What was that about liking his parents?

"Did you just say you love me?" His heart sped up.

She gazed at him with wide, pain-filled eyes. "You're my best friend, Brian. Of course, I love you." She placed a cold hand on his cheek.

His heart slowed again like a car now running out of gas.

They were back to friends. That was something. Better than nothing.

"I tried calling." He didn't know what to do with his hands. Or feet. Or face.

"And texting and emailing and writing." A tiny smile flickered, then was gone.

"Did you read my letter?"

"No."

Another stab of rejection pierced his heart.

"We need to talk, Brian. I want to have a simple, honest conversation."

He looked at the overnighter. "Are you planning to stay?"

"If I'm welcome." She suddenly seemed uncomfortable. "It's too late to fly out tonight. I can always—"

"You're always welcome to stay with me. Every day. All day. You are always welcome here."

"Thanks." She looked around again. "Have you eaten?"

"Huh?" How could she think of food at a time like this? He'd been hounding her for weeks, desperate for an explanation. Now she was here as if she dropped in all the time.

"You look awful. Like you haven't slept or eaten anything. I'm hungry. Take a shower while I order takeout. Do you want Chinese or pizza?"

He ran a hand over his jaw. She was right. His scruff was scratchy, and he was wearing yesterday's sweats.

Thoughts tumbling over and over, he headed down the hall to the bedrooms and bath.

"Hey, MechE."

He turned at the sound of his nickname.

"It'll be all right." Her smile was sad. "We've been friends for too long to let something like marriage ruin it."

He thought of the red velvet box in his top bureau drawer and then let go of his Christmas wish. At least they were still friends.

Brian wandered into the kitchen just as the Chinese food arrived.

Mel set the enormous paper bag on the kitchen counter and pulled out two bottles of water.

"I might need something stronger." He reached for a bottle of white wine.

She opened the first of four white cartons to scoop General Tsao's chicken onto their plates. "I thought we could chow like old times." She pointed at the coffee table with two double sheets of paper towel serving as placemats with a fork and spoon set on either side.

He opened a cabinet and grabbed two wine glasses and the bottle of wine, and returned to the living room, pushing the table way from the couch with his foot.

He lowered into a cross-legged position just as she set a plate in front of him. The sweet tang of the coated chicken made his stomach lurch, but he picked up his fork anyway.

"So?" He lifted a brow as a prompt. "What did you want to talk about?"

Chapter 11

*S*he settled on the floor next to him, running her hands over her thighs to dry her sweaty palms.

"I regret the way things ended between us at the resort."

God, she sounded so formal, like she was talking to her commanding officer. This wasn't what she rehearsed during the flight from San Antonio to Denver and again during the flight here.

He's your friend. Your bestie. MechE. Calm the heck down, Davenport.

"First, I want to say how sorry I am for walking out on you. Walking away wasn't fair. It's not something I do normally. And it's not something I'm proud of."

"Then why did you walk away?"

"I want you to know I don't care whether you take the job or not. Well, I do. It would be good for you to take it. I mean, I care because it's important to you."

"Mel?" He rested a warm hand on her thigh. "I'm listening. Take your time."

The stress in her body from the day of go-go-go to get here began to melt away. "I didn't leave because of your job. I left because I didn't want you to feel responsible for me. I kept hearing you say you couldn't stand the thought of watching me die and that you didn't think you could go on if you lost me."

She turned so she could see his face better. "That's when the what-ifs started. What if we had to make a choice between your job or mine? What if I gave up my military career for you and began resenting you? What if you gave up your opportunity and started resenting me?"

"But it wouldn't be like that. After all our years together, you should know that. What's really going on here, Mel?"

The pain in his eyes hurt so bad, her memory box of pain popped open and the contents flooded out.

"What if my cancer comes back and you can't handle it? What if you leave me?"

He sucked in a breath. His eyes widened. "You mean just like your dad left you? And just like your mom left you when she moved to Florida."

"You've always been my rock." Tears spilled over and trickled down her cheek. "I couldn't stand it if you left me."

"I'm not going to leave you."

"That's what my dad said"—a sharp sob escaped–"and he died when I needed him most." Waving her hand to hush him, she went on. "I know it wasn't his choice. It was an accident. But I've come to realize his death is the reason I've always kept people at arm's length, even those I love. If I don't let people into my life, then it won't hurt so much when they die."

"But it *will* hurt, Mel. Those people who cry the most at funerals cry because they have regrets. Regrets for not spending more time, or not having a life filled with wonderful memories. I don't want there to be any regrets between us. I want to love hard for the rest of my life, and I want you to be the one I love the most." He lifted her hand in his. "Mel, I would never choose my career over you. Without you, none of it matters anyhow."

She pressed her free hand against his lips. "You can talk when I'm done."

Her laugh was shaky. "I want to start by apologizing. I thought I was doing you this great favor. I thought I was saving you from having to make a choice between your dream job and me. I decided you were better off without me complicating your life."

He lifted to his knees, cradling her face between his hands. "Melissa, that has to be the stupidest thing I've ever heard come out of your mouth, and you are not a stupid woman. I don't care what kind of complications you come with. I love you, Melissa Alison Davenport, and I want to spend the rest of my life showing you, every single day, how much."

She blinked away tears. "Well, I'm not sure it's the stupidest thing I've ever said, but it might rank up there somewhere." She gazed deep into his emotional eyes. "My mom made me realize you have the right to choose for yourself whether or not you want to be with me. Just for the record, I've already made my choice."

"What is it?"

"I don't want to be your fiancée."

His breath hitched, and he began to pull away.

She grabbed his arm and held on. "But if the position of wife is still open, I'd like to fill that position for as long as life gives us."

His resistance evaporated. "Mel? Do you mean it?" He croaked out the words. "You don't know how bad I wanted—no, needed—to hear that." He grabbed her hand. "Are you sure?"

"One hundred and ten percent."

He took the ring box out of his pocket. "I decided in the

shower that, one way or another, I was going to do everything I could to show you I love you more than anything. And look, I'm already on my knees."

She giggled as he lifted her hand and slid the ring on her finger.

"No give-backs."

"Nope. No take-backs either." She laughed as pure happiness ran up her spine and zinged out to every toe and fingertip. "Merry Christmas, MechE."

"The first of many together, BestE." His warm lips pressed against hers. The kiss became more urgent, and he pressed harder with a promise of more.

She reluctantly pulled back. "If you don't have plans for the holidays, I promised your parents we'd fly back to Denver tomorrow. Weather permitting." She scooted onto the couch, tugging him to join her, snuggling in like a bear for a winter's nap.

"I'll fly with you anywhere, Mel."

"How about paradise?"

Brian twined their fingers together, and she admired the flash and glimmer of the engagement band.

"We're already there, love."

Thank you for reading Melissa and Brian's story. If you love mature, over forty romances, you might enjoy the rest of the Silver Fox Resort series novels. Check out all my books on my website, at LyzKelley.com

To keep tabs on Lyz's latest releases, connect with her by signing up for her newsletter. As a bonus you will get a **free book** in the Silver Fox Resort just for becoming a Kelley's Hero: https://geni.us/LyzKelleyFreeBook

Author Notes

Dear Readers,

If you have read any of my prior books, you know I loved to create unique characters. *Sweet December* came about when I read an article about the first U.S. female military fighter pilot, and my brain instantly started creating a story.

But there was a hesitation.

Even though I'm surrounded by former military serving friends and family, the challenge is I've never served. Sure, I can Google the layout of the military base in San Antonio, but I wouldn't know the layout of the building or what the place smells like, or how the personnel interact.

Luckily, a retired WSO (Weapons System Officer) helped me out. Not only did he fact check my work, but he got others involved as well. Because, after all, a writer must know if a certain type of aircraft can land on a regional airport runway and the time required to file a flight plan. {Grin}

The other reason I wanted to write this story is because I have friends in similar fields who have dedicated their lives to their career, but often speak to how lonely life can be.

Plus, I know couples who have paired up in order to travel and share their remaining years together.

All of these elements combined, I believed, would make a wonderful backdrop for Melissa and Brian.

So here's to companionship, love, and living a good life.

~Lyz

More Books By
Lyz Kelley

Do you want a free book?

I've got a present for my readers, your very own ebook exclusive.

https://geni.us/LyzKelleyFreeBook

Click Here

Sign up to start falling in love today!

Thank you for reading: SWEET
DECEMBER

Award-winning author Lyz Kelley mixes a little bit of heart, healing, humanity, happiness, honor, hope, and honor in all her books that are written especially for you.

She's is a total disaster in the kitchen, a compulsive neat freak, a tea snob, and adores writing about and falling in love with everyday heroes.

Please also consider leaving a review on Amazon Goodreads and/or BookBub. Reviews help readers find new books to read, and authors find their footing.

You can also find Lyz on Facebook and Instagram for news, contests, giveaways, and more exciting stuff!

Website
Newsletter Sign Up
Facebook
Instagram
Goodreads
BoodBub

Copyright

SWEET DECEMBER Copyright © 2021 Belvitri, LLC

Email: Lyz@LyzKelley.com
Newsletter Sign Up: www.LyzKelley.com
Facebook: www.facebook.com/LyzKelley
Instagram: https://www.instagram.com/lyzkelley/

or are used fictitiously, and any resemblance to the actual persons, living or dead, business establishments, events or locales is entirely coincidental. For questions and comments about the quality of this book please contact us at Lyz Kelley's contact page.

Cover Art: Covers by Maria Connor, Author Concierge